The Dance Centre Presents

COPPÉLIA

CHI VARNADO

OTHER BOOKS IN SERIES

The Dance Centre Presents Giselle

The Dance Centre Presents The Nutcracker

ALSO BY CHI VARNADO

The Old House In The Country

A Canyon Trilogy:
Life Before, During and After the Cedar Fire

The Tale of Broken Tail

GnomeWood Press
P.O. Box 404
Ramona, CA 92065
GnomeWoodPress.com

Cover illustration by Pam Wilder
Book cover and interior design by Monkey C Media
Edited by Adrianne Moch

First Edition
Printed in the United States of America

ISBN: 978-1-7341423-4-1 (Trade Paperback)
ISBN: 978-1-7341423-5-8 (E-Pub)

Library of Congress Control Number: 2021905557

For Helen and all who dream of dancing:

Dance through life with grace,
poise and purpose.

The Story of Coppélia

Coppélia is about a foolish young man who falls in love with a pretty doll named Coppélia. Franz, the young man, deserts his true sweetheart, Swanilda, who soon discovers her rival is just a doll. Changing into the doll's clothes, Swanilda fools the old toymaker who made Coppélia into thinking *she* is the doll. Through this trick, she saves Franz from one of the toymaker's evil schemes. Franz, realizing his foolishness, then asks Swanilda to forgive him, and the two are soon reunited.

DANCESPIRATION

Let dance happen wherever it strikes!

Why not dance our way through life? Easier said than done? Absolutely—at times. Especially during a pandemic, right? But hopefully, we can keep reminding ourselves that a dance studio is not the only place we may twirl. One can literally dance almost anywhere. I remember, years ago, after unloading hay out of the truck, one of my favorite songs was playing. I turned up the volume with the dashboard knob, and frolicked around the horse pasture. It felt fantastic! I leaped, turned and jumped in my own private dance party. While I had acres to cavort around in, dodging logs and gopher holes took some effort. But we can also dance in a grocery store aisle, under a tree in the park, or inside our house or apartment between the furniture. Get creative about it. So sometimes—just accept the challenge and dance wherever it strikes!

—Love,
Miss Chi

ADVANCE PRAISE FOR
THE DANCE CENTRE PRESENTS
COPPÉLIA

"The story of *Coppélia* continues to fascinate us with the day in and day out of our young ballet dancers living in a small town. Toggling between the historical stories of classical ballets, we are taken breathless by their movement while also being pulled into each character's struggles and triumphs of growing up in today's current events. Chi brings an honest understanding to the daily life of teenagers, framed around the grounding experience of being involved in an art form as a young person. We get to connect with the intimate experience between dance teacher (mentor, second parent, life coach, inspiration... maybe feminist role model?) and the young students trying to figure out how life works. It is summed up in one line, "This 'ballet family'... is much more diverse and broader than just dance."
—Erica Buechner, professional dancer/
choreographer in San Diego, CA and dance
teacher at Francis Parker School

"I love the book *Coppélia*! It tells a sweet story of dance and growing up. The message of not being afraid to advocate for what you believe in, even if you are young, and the importance of family, resonates with young readers. I will read this book over and over again for a long time."
—Justice Choate, Former ballet student
and currently attending college

"The Author has taken a ballet which debuted in Paris in 1870, and created a fascinating, modern story with dancing and interaction of young teens as they prepare for their futures!"

—Beverly Silvers, Former piano teacher

"*The Dance Centre Presents Coppélia* is an entertaining read that will keep you on your toes as the characters find their way through life with the help of dance."

—Helen Buchanan, UC Berkeley
student and ballet dancer

"The book was good. It had nothing that I would say is 'not appropriate' and that's good. I really like how the perspectives are different in every book. It was interesting to see Jack's life. I really liked it and thought it was just as good as the other ones."

—Olivia, Eleven-year-old ballet student

Contents

1

BLOW OUT

Jack

Dance with love in your heart.

Jack's right foot slams down onto the brake pedal as he steers sharply toward the direction he's skidding. It had all happened so fast. He braces himself against whatever impact might be coming and time slows down. He wonders if this could be it.

Just this morning, he'd gotten out of bed thinking this was simply going to be another typical Saturday. First—a shower; second—breakfast of champions: Wheaties, of course; and then getting ready for ballet class. The house was eerily quiet and he realized Dad must have already gone to the garage.

While Jack brushes his teeth, he stares at the reflection in the mirror and stops abruptly. There, as clear as all get-out, is his mother staring back at him. The hairs on the back of his neck rise, tears sting his eyes, and the galloping beat in his chest threatens to explode his whole body. How had he missed it before? Everyone tells him how much he resembles her, but he'd never seen it himself—until now. And it freaks him out.

Then he remembers. *Today* is the anniversary of Mom's death. How could he have forgotten? It's been seven years, but it still hits him like a freight train. Yet his life must go on. Ever since she'd passed away from that awful, brutal cancer, there's not a day goes by without him thinking about her. Jack's been pretty much left to his own devices—Dad has his own way of coping with grief. His work at the shop, fixing cars, still consumes him.

But yet—here she is now. Mom is part of him. He can see that now: her blue eyes, the ski-sloped nose, and her slightly freckled complexion. "I'll try to make you proud, Mom. I have no idea how, but I'll do my best." He takes one last look in the mirror, closes the bathroom door behind him, then the front door, and walks out to his car.

Tightening his grip on the steering wheel, which threatens to spin out of his hands, he's barely aware of the screeching tires. The front right corner of the car bumps, flops, and flaps—dipping down into the center of the rotation. Dust billows up all around the little old Honda as it slides into a smoky halt on the dirt pullout next to the road.

Finally realizing the worst is over, he exhales sharply and senses Mom's presence.

"Are you there?" He feels a gentle warmth, but his heart races. "Did you protect me?"

The sensation fades and he becomes aware of his hands, as if they are separate entities beyond his control. Slowly, his whitened knuckles come into focus, obscuring his tightly wrapped fingers around the steering wheel. It's almost like he has to will them open to let go. One-by-one he straightens the digits and flattens his hands. And then, suddenly, they come shaking toward his face and he leans into them.

What is happening to me, Mom? Nothing's going right. I'm a senior in high school—almost died here—and have no idea what I want to do when I grow up. Tears flood his eyes and he leans back into the seat, staring out the dirty windshield.

Eventually, Jack regains his composure and gets out of the car to assess the damage. He kicks the mangled right front tire in exasperation.

"Crappy, good-for-nothing, heap of junk! Why do I keep driving this?" He gives it another swift kick, then hops around in a circle holding his foot. After a few choice words, shouting at the blown-out tire, he pulls himself together again. He now calmly removes the spare and tools from the trunk, jacks up the car, and changes the tire. At least he can thank Dad for teaching him how to do that, along with oil changing and other minor repairs. He'd insisted that Jack work in the garage a couple afternoons a week, helping out, to at least gain a skill to fall back on if he ever needs to. Dad is all for him finding a path of his own, but in the meantime, he wants his son to be productive. Jack would really rather not work on cars at all. It's just not his thing. *What is my thing, though?*

❧

"Dude, you missed like the whole class, man!" Todd calls over to Jack as he comes into the studio.

"Yeah, why are you so late?" Randi asks, sitting under the ballet *barres*. "Miss Val thought she'd have to rearrange the order of our rehearsal today since you weren't here."

"It's a long story." Jack shakes his head and drops his dance duffle next to her.

Miss Val strides over to the desk and sets down her green spiral notebook. "We missed you at class. Did you oversleep?"

"I wish." Jack huffs at the memory and runs a hand through his dark brown mop, which now hangs well below his ears. "I had a blowout on the way here and then spun out."

"Oh my gosh, Jack! Are you all right—and your car?" Miss Val wrings her hands, concerned.

"Yeah, I'm okay—and the junkmobile. I should just get rid of it. It's like a death trap."

The group of Advanced dancers stare at him from the various places they're standing, stretching, or snacking. Class has just ended and they are about ready to start the Saturday morning rehearsal of *Coppélia*.

Todd saunters over and gives Jack a reassuring slap on the back. "Well, I'm glad you've arrived safely. Hey, can I bum a ride after?"

Jack laughs along with the rest of them. "Yeah, sure—but I'm tellin' ya—you're staking your life on the lousy tires of that junkyard jalopy." A grin eventually warms his face at the lightheartedness of his buddy. And he's happy to at last be together with his dancer friends, where they can now get swept away by the story of *Coppélia*. *Oh no, I'm beginning to sound like Randi and Paige and the whole "ballet family" thing.*

"Okay, Jack, now that we know you're okay—go ahead and warm up your ankles and do some light stretches. We'll need you pretty soon." Miss Val looks down at her choreography notebook and scrunches her dark eyebrows, presumably trying to decipher what she'd choreographed a week ago. "Let's start with you, Annie."

"For the friends dance?" Annie asks, walking upstage right toward her starting position.

"Yes. But besides being one of Swanilda's friends, I might need you to be the mayor who marries the couple. We'll see." Miss Val looks up from her notes and smiles. "You know what, Annie?"

"W-h-a-t—" she asks, uncertain.

As the silence prevails, they all turn attentively toward their teacher.

Paige giggles. "Uh-oh, is Miss Val having one of her strokes of genius? You do kind of have that look in your eye."

Finally answering, she lowers the hand holding the spiral notebook. "No—not really. I was just thinking how fortunate we are that Annie still chooses to join us, even though she's long since graduated and has her modeling jobs and college classes." She lifts her arms and hugs the book to her chest. "I just want you to know how much we appreciate you being here with us." Ever since the fire that destroyed their house and practically everything they owned, Miss Val is more nostalgic or grateful, or something.

"Aw, that's so sweet, Miss Val. Of course I'm here. I'd miss this place too much if I left for very long." Annie looks around at the group. "And you guys are great, too."

The class laughs while Jack grins from his place on the floor, stretching.

"Okay then—Swanilda, come on over here."

Randi *chassés* over to the corner to assume her lead role.

"Paige, you stand there." Miss Val points to the right of Annie. "And Brindle, Julie, and Sophia— follow behind them. Hey everybody? Remember the Dancespiration: Dance with love in your heart." Miss Val laughs. "I know it's kind of cheesy, but let's do it anyway. Keep in mind, you are all good friends of Swanilda and you're very happy for her upcoming wedding, yeah?"

"Okay, whatever you say, Miss Val." Paige gives Randi a sideways hug and laughs. "We got your back, Swanilda."

"All right then, enough of this sappy stuff. Let's get on with it."

They move into a v-formation and Miss Val has them travel across the diagonal with *assemblés*, *faillís*, and *tour jetés*. They each will follow their blissfully engaged friend, dutifully and joyfully.

Jack leans over his flexed left foot and a twinge shoots up his leg. He rotates his ankle and the feeling subsides. *It must be from kicking that blasted tire.* He watches the group of girls learn their dance and his ex-girlfriend, Marie, pops into his head. Suddenly, he's taken hostage by those hurt feelings he'd hoped were over with by now. But here they are again, not quite as raw as they were initially, but still painful. When some guy on the football team had shown an interest in her at the beginning of this school year, she'd left him behind, like an old castoff hat. At least that's what it felt like. *Why hadn't I seen the signs? She never really listened to me when other guys were around, flirting with them when she probably didn't know I was looking...* He senses Mom's presence again, just like after the accident, and wonders if he's going crazy. *Please—not here, not now.*

He changes legs, observing Randi and Paige skip around each other before changing partners, and notices how happy they all seem. The story of this ballet, *Coppélia*, has gotten him thinking about shallow attractions and how they sometimes can get you into trouble. Like when Franz, who he's playing, is enticed by another girl even though he's already engaged to Swanilda. The character becomes so infatuated he doesn't realize Coppélia is actually a doll—not even a real person!

"Jack. Hey, Jack! Are you ready?" Miss Val calls from her perch by the stereo.

He nods and tries to clear his mind for the task at hand. "Mm hmm." Standing up, he pops his neck right and then left as the group moves off to the side to practice their new steps. Deanne carries the chair from Miss Val's desk to the upstage right corner. Todd, as Dr. Coppelius, the toymaker, stands there waiting for her.

"So much for being a gentleman and carrying my chair," Deanne says, setting it down directly in front of him.

"Excuse me, please. That's kind of in my way." Todd sneers sarcastically. "Now I have to walk *all* the way around it."

"Oh please." Deanne plops herself down in the seat and puts her feet wide apart, making herself as large an obstacle as possible.

With overly dramatic motions, Todd lumbers slowly around her and fakes exhaustion by the time he gets around her.

"Such drama, you guys," Randi says, giggling from the other side of the studio.

"No kidding." Jack agrees. But he's not really in the mood for this today.

Miss Val walks over, pointing behind Deanne. "You start back there, remember?"

Todd scratches his head, feigning confusion. "Oh yeah. I do, don't I?"

Jack walks over to stage left to begin his dance of eyeing and flirting with Coppélia, the doll whom his character is smitten with. Todd works the magic of Dr. Coppelius while Franz falls hopelessly in love. Jack tries, but nothing's making sense right now—after his near-death experience this morning.

2

Rehearsing Coppélia

Julie

When in doubt, dance!

Julie sits on the bed watching anime on her laptop, an ordinary Saturday morning. Before moving here last year, the group of kids she hung out with had all talked about their favorite series and given each other recommendations. But here in Nuevo, she hasn't found anyone who shares these interests. She misses her old friends—however, she can still enjoy some of what they had all shared together. Without any *real* friends here yet, this enjoyable activity at least allows her to pass the time. With a new baby in the house, her parents have been more preoccupied and busier.

Even though Valentine's Day was almost two weeks ago, she's enjoying this particular episode because it reminds her of that holiday. She loves artsy stuff like this, and anything holiday related. Multicolored, animated butterflies fill the screen and they fly hither and thither across a beautiful, magical sky. The Japanese soundtrack adds to the ethereal world that is becoming Julie's hideaway space she escapes to more often these days. The boy points to the butterfly he believes is his, but keeps changing his mind until one transforms into another. *How do they do that? It's so cool!*

Julie glances to the right side of the screen when a balloon appears out of nowhere. The characters in the basket drift through the clouds and try to figure out their next plan of action. The high-pitched dialogue rises in volume with their growing concern for the safety of all those butterflies. Each lovely creature is fervently trying to attract a suitable mate.

Mom pokes her head in the doorway, knocking gently on the wall. "Julie, how about turning that off and getting breakfast so you won't be late for ballet."

"I will in a minute, Mom. I promise."

Julie's focus returns to the point in the story where only a few "singles" are left. The kids in the basket keep trying to give one particular butterfly advice, but circumstances keep blocking its success.

Julie hears the baby cry and Mom passes by again. "Now, Julie."

She reluctantly closes the computer, opens the dresser drawer containing leotards and tights, and quickly gets dressed. After selecting her favorite purple kimono and bright pink Crocs, she grabs her ballet bag and heads to the kitchen. The baby is now screaming louder than she thought possible for an infant. Her younger sister, by almost fifteen years, was a surprise to all three of them. Little Cari's howling does not stop when Mom rocks the baby carrier perched on the counter. Her mother's hair sticks out sideways from a messy ponytail. Bloodshot eyes make her look like a homeless person, as she clutches her cup of coffee and leans heavily on her elbows.

I wish Dad was here more to help out. I kind of miss having both parents to myself. Wait, that seems overly selfish, but it is how I feel—sometimes. They're both so distracted these days. Her father, as a busy airline pilot, has an erratic home schedule. Julie slices a poppy seed bagel in half and pops it into the toaster before selecting a small container of blueberry yogurt to go with it.

Mom picks up the baby and carries her out of the room. "Ten minutes, honey!"

"Okay." Julie powers through breakfast then brushes her teeth and the three of them leave the house and head to the Dance Centre.

The girls mark through what they already know of "the friends dance." Of course, Randi fits the role of Swanilda perfectly: smart, pretty, calculating. Earlier in the rehearsal, Julie had watched her learn the part where she tricks her *fiancé*, Franz, into believing she is actually the doll in the window above the street. She'd batted her eyes and smiled flirtatiously with conviction.

"All right, are you girls ready?" Miss Val carries her notebook to front center and Swanilda's friends gather around Randi to pick up the new choreography where they'd left off on Tuesday.

Julie adjusts her leotard back down for the umpteenth time. She's tired of getting wedgies. *I guess I'd better retire this old thing and start wearing my new long-sleeved black one. It is colder now.* She squints when a shaft of sunlight reflects off the mirrors lining the front wall of the studio and moves accordingly. It's a bright, crisp February day and because the large window shades are pulled up, the natural light bathes the studio in a warm glow, making it cozy and inviting inside while the cars gleam in the parking lot outside.

"Randi—I need you on stage left." Miss Val points. "And let's have Sophia and Julie over there. Annie, Brindle, and Paige—how about the three of you circle toward that corner and prepare to move across the diagonal."

The dancers follow these new instructions for the first time. Delibes' lively music inspires their *pas de chats, chassé en tournants, soutenu turns,* and *petite jetés.* Julie's heart lifts, like she really is one of Swanilda's friends, back in that festive village a century and a half ago. The story line comes to her in snippets, off and on, as they rehearse.

Coppélia *is about a foolish young man who falls in love with a pretty doll named Coppélia. Franz, the young man, deserts his true sweetheart, Swanilda, who soon discovers her rival is just a doll. Changing into the doll's clothes, Swanilda fools the old toymaker who made Coppélia into thinking she is the doll. Through this trick, she saves Franz from one of the toymaker's evil schemes. Franz, realizing his foolishness, then asks Swanilda to forgive him, and the two are soon united again.*

When Miss Val finally calls an end to the rehearsal, the tired but gratified dancers move *en masse* to the *barres,* grab waters from their bags underneath, and gulp in silence.

Sophia screws the lid back onto her bottle, turning to Julie. "It seems longer than a month since the Women's March, doesn't it?"

"It does." Julie agrees.

"Not to me." Randi tosses her silver thermos into her bag. "Everything's going way too fast—it just means high school will be over far too soon for Paige and me. We'll be in college before we know it."

Paige laughs. "I know, but I really am looking forward to going to Berkeley." She sits down to untie her *pointe* shoes.

Even though Julie is now a sophomore, she feels much younger than the others. *Is it because I'm the newest one in the class?* "I thought the Women's March was interesting and I'm so glad I got to go. With a new baby in our house, I don't get to do as much anymore. Thanks for taking me."

Sophia wipes the water off her chin and nods. "*De nada.* It was definitely more fun with you there than it would have been with just my mom and me."

"I couldn't believe how many people were there," Brindle says. "Didn't you think it was crowded, too, Mom?"

Miss Val rifles through her briefcase and looks over at the group. "It was—but that's good. The more people get involved with these issues the better."

Deanne hoists a magenta tote over her shoulder when she sees her mom's car pull up outside. "Bye, guys. See ya later."

The girls wave to her and watch Jack and Todd come back from the convenience store at the other end of the small strip mall and get into Jack's little beat-up Honda.

Paige faces the group. "I especially liked the speech that one woman gave, about how our social justice affects everyone—or something like that."

Brindle stands up, carefully ducking her head to avoid hitting the *barres*. "And also honoring the legacy of all those movements that came before and are still going on."

"Yeah, like the Civil Rights Movement, Occupy Wall Street, and Black Lives Matter," Sophia says.

Julie thinks of one more to add. "Don't forget the suffragettes!"

"Absolutely! It's only been a hundred years since women earned the right to vote." Paige shakes her head. "Progress, huh?"

Julie's mom appears at the open studio door, holding the baby. "You ready, Julie?"

She nods and the group turns toward the bundle in Mom's arms.

"Ooh, can I see her?" Randi scurries over to peer into the pink blanket. "She's so tiny—and *so* precious."

Mom smiles and Julie joins them.

"Her voice isn't tiny, though." Julie grins at her little sister and wiggles the sock-covered toes sticking out the bottom of the blanket. "But we love her anyway."

"Yes, we do," Mom says and leans down to kiss Cari's forehead.

Miss Val approaches with open arms. "May I?"

"Of course." Mom gently places the baby in their teacher's hands and a smile, or grimace—it's hard to tell with an infant, takes over the miniature face.

Miss Val sways back and forth to the soft music still playing on the stereo, stepping back to allow more space for movement. She dances slowly, waltzing next to the group with abbreviated steps.

Randi laughs. "Do you ever stand still, Miss Val?"

Finishing with one more gradual turn, she hands the baby back and shrugs. "I don't know. Maybe when I'm asleep?"

The group laughs and Julie grabs her sweater to leave. *These girls are super nice. I'm sure glad we found this studio.*

∾❦∾

After dinner, Julie stands up to clear the table while Mom puts the baby to bed. "Is Dad still coming home tomorrow?"

"Mm hmm, as long as the weather holds up back East."

"The usual, huh? I don't think I'd like living there and having to deal with all that snow."

Mom scoops little Cari out of the carrier. "Well, there are tradeoffs, I suppose. It can be really beautiful there in the spring and summer—especially in upstate New York. At least that's what I've heard." Mom starts to leave, but turns back. "Just try not to watch too much anime tonight, okay?"

Julie can't help but roll her eyes, slightly annoyed. "I won't." She collects the plates and takes them to the sink as Mom carries her sister off to bed. Rinsing the dishes and loading the dishwasher, she starts thinking about which episode she's going to watch next. *Too much anime? What does that even mean—how many episodes is that? Who decides? Doesn't Mom realize how much I miss my friends and how my anime is about the only thing I* can *do—since we hardly ever go out to* do *anything anymore?* All Julie knows is that she can barely wait. It helps tune out the baby's crying. She can already hear her starting. Again.

3

THE JALOPY

Jack

Sometimes—pressing downward is just as important as lifting up.

"The dude can seriously turn," Todd says, leaning toward Jack. "And look at all the girls—they're practically drooling."

Jack crosses his arms across his chest and grins half-heartedly. "Yeah, but check it out—he's not even all the way up on his toes. And his knees are bent."

"Are you kidding me? You notice *that*?"

Jack glances toward Todd, but then returns his focus to the guest teacher in their dance productions class at school. "Just sayin'." His ballet training gives him a discerning eye regarding technique. The importance of *turnout* and correct alignment is engraved into his body movements.

"Okay, everybody!" The instructor claps his hands and tells them to try the new combination.

The students step forward, spacing themselves, and the heavy bass pulses them into action.

"Five, six, seven, eight. Turn to the right!" Boom, boom, boom, boom. "Pick it up, guys. Let's see it now—here comes the layout!" Thrum, thrum, thrum, thrum. "There you go. You got it!"

The group continues moving to the hip hop beat and the teacher's commanding instructions. They finish the pattern with an outside turn, in parallel, which Jack detests. He ends up pulling off an extra tour, with *turnout* and flair.

"Showoff." Todd razzes his friend as the females in class continue to fawn over the instructor.

The bell rings, marking the end of class, and the school day. The students give the guest teacher a round of applause and take off for the locker rooms.

"Hey, can I bum a ride to ballet? My bike has a flat tire so I left it at home."

"Instead of fixing it?" Jack teases. "Sure, but what if I hadn't been here today? What would you have done then?"

"You're always here, man. Let's go."

Jack grabs the *barre* as he finishes the double outside *pirouette*, staying up *en relevé* at the end. *Not like that jazz teacher earlier. I know it's a different dance form, but still—technique is technique.*

"Good job, Jack. Do you want to go for a triple next time?" Miss Val smiles as she moves on to help Paige with her spot.

After another round of *pirouettes*, the students carry the portable *barres* over to the side of the studio and take a water break. Miss Val uses the time to go over choreography notes.

"Hey, Annie—is that a new car you drove here today?" Sophia asks. "It's super cute."

"And sporty," Julie adds.

"It is!" A big smile takes over Annie's face. "I just got it this weekend."

Jack looks out the large window and sees the shiny, red Toyota sedan right out front. "Is that it?" He points outside.

"Uh huh. I love it!"

In the parking lot, Jack sees the mixed array of colored hunks of metal in the subdued gray afternoon. It makes him think, somehow, of perspective and what might be beautiful to some is downright ugly to others. He notices a shift in his preference. *Each of these currently functioning, individual transports will end up in the landfill someday. Then what? Just buy another one and then throw it away when it wears out. But what then? When will we run out of space for trash?* He's starting to question how sustainable such a practice is in the long run. *Isn't anyone thinking about that?*

Miss Val calls them all over to start rehearsing one of the village scenes, the one where Jack, as Franz, becomes enamored with the doll in the window. *Do all these story ballets feature such dunces for men?* He thinks back to when he danced the part of Albrecht in *Giselle. He was a reckless dude who led a poor peasant girl on even though he was already engaged. Some guys might think that's okay, but it's dishonest. Integrity should account for more than it seems to these days, or back then.*

Jack moves to his place and Deanne sits primly in a chair, upstage right, behind, as of yet, a nonexistent large window frame. She has a demure, unchanging smile plastered on her face—as required for the part as Coppélia. The townspeople festively mingle and he dances here and there: waltzing with his *fiancé,* Swanilda; flirting with the doll—from the street in front of the window; carousing with his little buddies (a couple boys from the Intermediate class who will eventually join him in rehearsals). The lively, engaging music of this ballet works its magic and sweeps him into the realm of the story. And he lets it, as they all do, because *this* is what these dancers at the Dance Centre do every spring. They become one with the fairy tale.

When Brindle opens the door to leave with Deanne and Sophia—the three musketeers—a pitter patter of raindrops competes with the musical notes coming from the opposite corner of the studio. The Beginning class trickles in, bringing wet umbrellas and jackets to take the place of the Advanced dancer's ballet bags stashed under the *barres*. Miss Val looks over from her desk and welcomes the motley crew of youngsters.

"You ready? I have to hurry because Dad needs my help at the shop today." Jack pulls on his second shoe and heads for the exit.

"All right, already." Todd trots after him, trying to stuff his black, kinky hair into an uncooperative beanie and gives up halfway out the door.

Jack settles into the driver's seat of his small gray car and turns the key expectantly, trying to remain hopeful. It had trouble starting this morning, but this time it's a complete no go. "Blast. Not again!"

"I thought you fixed this thing," Todd says.

"Huh? I'm continuously fixing this thing. It doesn't seem to understand the condition of *being fixed*." He huffs loudly and stares at the unresponsive key in the ignition. "I'm really starting to hate this."

Todd opens the door to get out. "Sorry, dude. I'm gonna see if I can hitch a ride with Annie before she leaves." A wicked grin flashes across his face. "She's got a *new* car."

The door rattles shut, and Jack takes a deep breath, closes his eyes, and leans back. Not long after, he reaches back to fetch his phone from the rear seat. *Maybe Dad can send someone over to give me a jump.*

Dad apologizes for not being able to come to the rescue right away, so Jack figures he ought to try to get some of his homework done while waiting. Deciding on economics, he pulls the heavy book from his backpack and flips through the chapters rather absentmindedly. Large and small, light and bold text swims across the faded pages and images float as he loses focus. A graph captures his attention, so he scrutinizes it further.

What's that bar supposed to represent anyway? He reads the fine print. *Hmm—why has mass transit use in the US declined in the last few years? Don't people know oil is a limited resource and it's filthy for the environment?* Jack scans the parking lot and stares at all the vehicles around him. Then he looks at the dirty dashboard of his own little Honda and groans. *What is it with our obsession of the almighty car, anyway?*

Jack startles awake when a big motorcycle roars through the lot. He hadn't even realized he'd dozed off. *I guess econ can do that to a person.* The rain is now coming down harder and moisture is blowing in the side window. It doesn't close all the way—so that's another thing that's wrong with this car. He decides to go back in the studio after Dad texts that he'll come as soon as he closes the shop.

He slips inside and sinks under the *barres* to watch the ballet class. *Wow, these aren't the Beginners. I must have slept through that whole class because these kids look older.* And Jack realizes *this* class is almost over when they spread out to do the *reverence* that will end it!

After Miss Val dismisses the group, she looks over at him. "What are you still doing here? Or did you go and come back?"

"No, I'm *still* here. My stupid car wouldn't start and my Dad can't come 'til he's done at work."

"I see." Miss Val starts putting attendance cards and papers into her briefcase and other things away in the desk. "You've been having a time with that car lately, haven't you?"

"Yes—unfortunately. Honestly—I think I'd be better off with *no* car than the one I have. At least my bike was more reliable."

After she covers the stereo with the pink dust cloth, she returns and asks if he'd like her to jump start his car with her truck.

"No, that's okay. Dad should be here pretty soon."

"Okay." She takes her sweater from the back of the chair and puts it on. "How's school going? Are you ready to be done yet—since you *are* a senior now— you know, spring fever and all?"

Jack ponders the question. "Yes and no, I guess. I mean, I'll miss my friends, but I am kind of over it. It's pretty boring."

Miss Val laughs. "Well, I'm here to tell you that college is *way* better than high school, at least it sure was for me."

"Like how?"

She turns the chair sideways and sits to face him, leaning back. "Hmm. For one thing, most everyone *wants* to be there instead of *having* to be there. And the classes are more interesting." She pauses in thought. "Maybe that's because the students, and probably the teachers as well, are more interested in the topics. Everyone seems to have a vested interest in the outcome of their studying, or their job."

They both glance toward the windows when a truck revs its engine. Jack's thoughts return to the graph in his textbook.

"You know, I was reading my econ book earlier and it said something about how public transportation is used less and less here in the US. Everybody *needs* their cars these days."

Miss Val chuckles, nodding her head toward the noisy truck. "It's also a status symbol for some."

Jack laughs, too. "For sure, especially in a small town like Nuevo, huh?"

"Yes indeed. Hey, have you seen the articles in the paper about the meeting coming up regarding widening the highway coming into town? Everybody seems to be clamoring for it, but I'm not so sure."

"Really? I haven't heard anything about it. That's all we need—more cars coming into town."

"Everyone is saying how growth is inevitable—that we need to prepare for it. My husband and I don't really agree, though. That kind of view does not lend kindly to sustainability." She shakes her head in disappointment.

"We've been studying the 2008–2009 recession in my class and talking about how the big financial institutions crumbled. All those bad loans people couldn't pay back and then lost their homes." He shrugs his shoulders.

"Then *those big businesses* got the bailouts while the people suffered. I think when anything gets too big, and no one person can possibly see the whole picture, then eventually it—or something—is bound to fail. No one is accountable and there's a sickening lack of integrity. It's just mind-boggling." Miss Val pulls her sweater around her tightly as if just now feeling the cold.

Headlights flash in the window and Jack stands up. "I guess my dad's here."

Miss Val pushes the chair back under the desk. "Well, let me know what you learn about the public transportation thing. I'm curious to hear more."

"Will do," he says as he opens the door for her and they each head out for the night. Jack and his dad manage to get the car started and back to the shop, where it will wait for its next procedure.

4

NEW FRIENDSHIP

Julie

Take care of your support system—be it friends, family, or your supporting leg.

The bell rings, and Julie slips the geography textbook into her backpack and puts on the sweater from the back of her chair. She glances down at her phone and scrolls through her Instagram feed for the latest activity. The familiar anime images flood her with both anticipation and a sense of connection. Not having any real close friends since moving here last year makes her all the more eager to find solace online. *At least there's this I can count on.*

After visiting her locker to exchange books for lunch, Julie notices Sophia sitting alone on the cement steps of the quad. She doesn't usually see her at school at all, except during P.E. sometimes—if all three classes meet for attendance and calisthenics on the outdoor basketball courts. *She looks kind of sad there, all by herself.* Sophia leans sideways into her elbow, staring off into space holding a half-eaten sandwich.

"Hey," Julie says, climbing the stairs toward her. "May I join you?"

Sophia straightens up and grins. "Sure, if you'd like to."

"Thanks. What's in your lunch today?" Julie sets down the sack and buttons her sweater. "Brrr. It's getting colder."

"PB&J. How 'bout you?" Sophia zips her bright yellow jacket and Julie settles in beside her.

"I've got yogurt with granola and some carrots." Julie opens the top of her bag and peers in. "And a chocolate bar! Where'd that come from? Hmm, Mom must have snuck it in when I wasn't looking."

"That sounds good." Sophia rewraps the rest of her sandwich and puts it back into her backpack. "I'm not that hungry."

Julie pulls the lid off the yogurt container and looks over at Sophia. "Are you okay?"

The quiet girl goes back to staring off into space in silence, for a little longer than is comfortable. "Not really—*mi abuela* is sick and I'm worried about her."

"Your grandmother?" Julie's taking Spanish this semester and the word sounds familiar.

"Mm hmm. We just found out she has cancer." A solitary tear rolls down her cheek.

"I'm so sorry, Sophia." Julie puts a hand on her shoulder. "Does she live nearby?"

"Sort of. She lives in Tijuana with my uncle's family."

"Well—" She's not sure what to say. "It's good she's with family, right? And Tijuana isn't that far away, is it?"

"No, but crossing the border takes forever now."

Julie looks across the quad and takes her first spoonful of yogurt. She pictures this old woman, sick in bed, with the family looking over her and feeding her spoonfuls of porridge—or something. When Julie goes for her second scoop, the lumpy yellow goop in the container no longer looks appetizing. After snapping the lid back in place, she digs around in the sack and pulls out the chocolate bar. When she starts unwrapping it, Sophia looks over.

"Want some?" Not waiting for a response, Julie peels off the wrapper and hands her a few squares. "Here, it's good medicine, *and* it's good for you."

Sophia's eyes sparkle, accepting the gift. "Why, is it dark chocolate?"

"Of course. Only the best for you," Julie teases.

As the girls savor the treat, they watch two guys toss a football back and forth at the bottom of the sunken quad. When one of them fumbles and drops the ball, a cheerleader scrambles forward to retrieve it. The girl runs up the stairs on the far side, laughing loudly.

The other guy, the one who threw it, bellows, "Hey, bring it back, Lacy!"

"No can do!" she shouts back.

The one who'd dropped the ball shakes his head and jogs slowly after her.

Julie returns her focus to Sophia. "How long has it been since you've seen her? Your grandmother, I mean."

"We went to see her last weekend. She seems so weak now. All she did was sit around the whole time we were there. And *she's* usually the one who's always busy in the kitchen, cooking for everyone."

"That must have been hard seeing her like that." Julie watches the guy return with the ball. "Do you know when you'll get to see her again?"

"Hopefully in a couple weeks—next time my dad can get both Saturday and Sunday off so we can spend the night and not have to come back the same day."

"Yeah, that makes sense." Julie gets up to throw away the trash and her phone pings. Instinctively, she picks it up, anticipating another Instagram notification. *Life and Hiccup* flashes across the screen in bold letters, announcing the release of the brand-new movie. Her heart rate quickens and she looks down at Sophia. "Hey, do you like anime?"

"What?" Sophia looks confused.

"Do you like to watch anime? I mean, there's a new movie that's just premiering now. Maybe you've heard of it—*Life and Hiccup?*"

"Huh? No, I don't think so."

Julie starts telling her about some of the anime shows she watches and how "awesome" they all are. "This new movie has been in the works for a long time and I can't wait to see it!"

"What's it about?"

"Well, it's kind of strange. They haven't spilled much of the plot yet, but the same writer *and* director have done several other movies that won lots of awards."

"But isn't it weird that no one knows what it's even about?"

"Mm hmm." Julie tries to find more information about it on her phone, but nothing comes up. "Who knows? Maybe it's so *hush hush* because so few anime movies are shown in theaters. But I'm guessing Life and Hiccup are the two main characters, but they haven't even given *that* away. Do you think you might want to go see it with me? It's playing only at one place that shows alternative films. How about this weekend?"

"Maybe. I'll have to see." Sophia takes a drink from her water bottle and the bell rings, ending their lunch break.

Julie picks up her things and turns to leave. "See you at ballet."

"Okay," Sophia answers and they head off in opposite directions.

Julie pushes the stroller over the bumpy path leading to their front door. When she bends down to check if her little sister is still asleep, the baby wakes up and starts to fuss. *Drat.* "Why can't you ever *stay* asleep, Cari? We could all use a break sometimes, you know?" She unbuckles the belt and scoops her up, leaving the stroller on the porch. "I sure hope dinner's ready. I'm starving."

Cari announces their arrival into the kitchen and Mom takes her. Julie goes to the sink to wash her hands and is relieved when she sees the pans on the stove are already turned off.

"Dinner's ready. Go ahead and dish yours up while I go change the baby. She smells way overdue."

Julie grabs a plate and helps herself to the breakfast-for-dinner meal: bacon, scrambled eggs, and toast. *It'll do. At least it's warm.* She hadn't realized how chilly she'd gotten outside. When Mom returns, Cari seems a little happier, so she puts her in the carrier in the center of the table. Julie rocks the baby so Mom can get her dinner.

When all three are at the table, either eating or somehow pacified, Mom's phone rings and she takes it into the living room. Cari's eyes track her as she leaves and big sister rocks the cradle some more. "That's a good baby." Rock, take a bite, rock, sip some milk, rock, coo at the infant....

Mom comes back into the kitchen and sets her phone on the counter. "That was Dad. His next flight got cancelled, so he'll be coming home tonight." As she takes her first bite, Cari starts fussing again. Mom groans, but scoops her up to hold for the rest of supper.

"Hey, Mom?"

"Hmm?" Mom hums to the baby while chewing.

"That new movie I told you about comes out this weekend. May I go see it—and take Sophia, from ballet?"

"Is she interested in anime?" Mom's eyes don't leave the baby.

"I don't know, but we talked about it and she might want to go. How about Saturday, after ballet?"

Mom closes her eyes and rocks back and forth with Cari.

"Well?" Julie finally says after a long pause.

"Hmm?"

"The movie, Mom. Can I go?"

"Not this weekend, honey. Dad will be here, and he specifically asked for family time."

"But Mom?"

"Maybe next weekend, Julie. You need to learn to wait sometimes," Mom snaps. "I'm sorry. I'm just so tired. I know you miss your old friends, but I'm starting to worry about how much time you're spending in front of a screen."

Julie rolls her eyes, but obediently gets up to clear the table and load the dishwasher. *Seriously? My screen time? What else am I supposed to do?"*

Outside the large windows a cold rain falls, while inside heat radiates from the perspiring dancers' bodies. Julie breathes hard as she leaps across the diagonal with Sophia and Brindle: *sauté, tombé, glissade, saut de chat.* Then the group *ballet runs* (right arm forward and left arm out—in this case) around to the back right corner (upstage right). As soon as the other side passes, they cross the opposite diagonal with *piqué arabesque, step through, double piqué turn, three chaînés turns,* and *finish with a relevé en attitude.*

"Good job, everyone!" Miss Val calls out as they end the piece in a center pose. "Don't forget to practice your parts at home. Hey, and also, visualize the steps when you lie in bed waiting for sleep to arrive. Maybe you'll get lucky and dream them into memory!"

"Or have nightmares about it and forget everything," Todd jokes.

The class laughs and Paige teases. "Do you always have to be so contrary?"

He crosses his arms and sticks his nose up in the air. "No."

Miss Val comes to his rescue. "But we love him anyway." She raises her shoulders and makes a funny face at the group.

"And we love you, too, Miss Val." Todd teases back and the class laughs again and prepares to leave.

As Julie walks toward the *barres* she catches up to Sophia. "Sorry about not being able to go to the movie today. Do you think you could go next weekend?"

Sophia grabs her phone and checks her calendar. "We're not going to Tijuana, so maybe, if I don't have too much homework. I can't believe how much they pile on when you get to high school. And I have to start reading *To Kill A Mockingbird*. But it's so hard to read anything right now—on top of all my other assignments."

Paige overhears. "I thought that was a great book. It even won the Pulitzer Prize."

"It's one of those timeless books," Brindle pipes up.

"Is there any book you don't like, Paige?" Randi asks, sliding over her ballet bag with a foot.

Paige pauses. "Well, I don't much care for those trashy romance novels."

"Hey—they're not *all* bad," Randi argues.

They all chuckle in unison. A few make their exit into the rainy afternoon while the conversation continues.

"I miss reading things like *The Giver*," Sophia says as she unties her *pointe* shoes.

"May I?" Julie reaches for one of the pretty, pink satin shoes and Sophia hands it to her to examine.

Brindle tosses her own pair into a pile. "That was a wonderful book—another timeless one."

Deanne gets up when her mother pokes her head in the door. "Bye, guys."

They all wave, and Paige brings up how Jonas in *The Giver* sure had to make some hard choices, when he had no options to begin with.

"That's definitely true," Jack says as walks out with Todd.

Julie agrees. "I'm glad we have the right to choose our own livelihoods, for the most part anyway."

"Yeah, me, too." Sophia takes back her shoe and puts it into her tote.

As they all get up to leave, Miss Val calls Julie over to the desk.

She says goodbye to her friends and joins the teacher. *I wonder what it's about.*

"Well, Julie," Miss Val begins. "How would you like to start *pointe*? I think you're ready. Of course, you'll have to stay on the *barre* this semester, and you won't be able to wear them in our concert. But you could at least start training—if you want to."

Julie's heart skips a beat. "Of course, I would! Thank you, Miss Val."

"Good. When your mom gets here, we can talk specifics and you'll be on your way."

Julie hurries over and gets her things ready to go. *I'm so excited! Maybe no movie today, but I'm getting toe shoes!*

5

BUILDING

Jack

Like everything in life, a dancer is built from a strong foundation.

The health of Jack's car continues to worsen. Besides that blowout where he'd spun out of control, the troublesome symptoms of the aging vehicle are growing in number. He'd had to replace the old spark plug wires, a malfunctioning fuel injector, the dead battery, and a leaky radiator, and now it seems the dirty carburetor has chosen to die in the middle of town.

Addressing his car, he sputters, "That's it—I'm done with this scrapheap of metal. This is the last time I'm going to deal with getting you towed and then just doing another temporary fix." He calls Dad from the side of the road. "Just haul it to the junkyard instead of back to the garage for even more repairs. And put it out of its misery!"

"But son, these cars can last forever if you just keep working on them." He pauses, then adds, "And you keep learning more mechanical skills each time, don't you think?"

Jack huffs and kicks the front right tire, which lacks a hubcap. "But I don't want to anymore, Dad. I spend practically *all* my free time in the shop and I'm not really that interested anymore. I'd like to learn other things *besides* how to work on cars."

"Like what?" Dad asks.

"I don't know—yet. I guess I'd just like to have time to figure out what it might be."

Now there's a huff on the other end of the line. "Okay then, I guess that means you'll be back on your bike for a while." He clears his throat. "Hang tight. I'll be there in about fifteen minutes."

Miss Val starts the music again for the village scene where Franz, i.e., Jack, becomes enamored with the doll, Coppélia. Deanne sits primly in her chair, pretending to hold a book and read. *She's pretty good at playing this part. She's kind of a flirt anyway.* Jack shows off with *brisés, grand jetés,* and grandiose gestures of both the balletic and pedestrian varieties. As he blows mock kisses to her, he's reminded a little of how he felt when Marie left him. He hadn't been ready for that and had pretty much begged her to stay with him. In a way, he'd blown kisses at Marie's shadow, trying to win her back—but she was long gone. And now, here he is playing the part again, except pretending. *What sad sacks we males can sometimes be—continually being blindsided and outwitted by the females of our species.*

"Jack, put some feeling into it!" Miss Val shouts over the music. "It's got to look like you're falling for her."

Todd bellows, "Yeah, man! You gotta fall for the doll!"

Jack laughs and ups the ante. "Hey—*you're* the character who can't catch a real one so you have to *make* the dolls!"

The class laughs, but Miss Val pulls them back on track so they won't have to start all over again. After running through a few of the other dances, the rehearsal ends and the dancers disperse. Jack looks out the large window beyond the *barres* at the sunny Saturday afternoon and remembers he has his bicycle outside. He's surprised how good that makes him feel. *I guess I must have had an ongoing worry about breaking down in the car, but now all I sense is relief. I can definitely live with this.*

Miss Val peers outside. "Where's your car, Jack?"

"It's long gone. I got tired of it constantly falling apart and decided to use my bike instead."

"From now on?"

"Yup." He smiles, reliving the *good riddance* state. "This is much more reliable."

"Good for you, Jack. You guys live pretty close to town anyway, don't you?" She puts the attendance cards into the manila folder and deposits it into her briefcase on the desk as Jack nods. Miss Val changes the subject and asks about college. "Do you know what you might be interested in studying next year? Are you going to the community college?"

"Yeah. It's all my dad and I can really afford and I'm not even sure what I want to major in yet."

The teacher sits down on the floor, joining him, and leans forward to stretch her back. "Well, you don't *really* need to know that yet. There are a lot of general education classes you'll have to take." She straightens up and arches back, looking at the ceiling. When she returns to normal posture, Miss Val smiles. "You could actually take something fun each semester, too. Who knows, it might help you find out what you'd be interested in."

"Hmm—that's true. I hadn't thought of that before."

"It's what I did at first—I guess just to make sure it really was *dance* I wanted to stick with."

"Was there anything else you might have done?" Jack can't imagine his ballet teacher as anything else.

Miss Val turns thoughtful. "Oh, maybe. But I realized I was interested in so many things, that eventually it made more sense to just get my degree in dance and follow my other interests outside of the college realm." She extends her long legs, crossing them at the ankles and leans back onto her hands.

This new bit of information piques Jack's curiosity. "Hmm. What else are you interested in?"

She smiles mischievously. "Construction—for one thing."

His jaw drops. "Construction? You mean like building stuff?"

She chuckles. "Mm hmm. And designing."

"Like architecture?"

"Yes." Her eyes twinkle with excitement.

"O-k-a-y—and what are you doing about that now, Miss Val?" he teases.

"Well, I actually designed our house and I'm the one registered as 'owner/builder' for our cabin. I figured nobody *really* knows about building with logs here in San Diego County. And we save money by not hiring a contractor. I serve as the general on it and hire out as needed."

By now, Jack's head is spinning. "How did I not know any of this about you?" He shakes his head in disbelief. "Not your typical ballet teacher, huh?"

They both laugh.

He knows where Miss Val and her family were living last year, after the fire, because the Advanced dancers had gone over to help work on props for *The Nutcracker*. But he isn't clear about where their property they're rebuilding on is. "How is your log cabin coming along?"

"Right now, we're framing interior walls and installing windows—it's getting tricky finding enough help, though." She settles down onto her back and pulls a knee to her chest.

She looks beat. I wonder if she'd let me help. "Hey, I need a job. And I'm not exactly *not* handy."

Miss Val perks up. "Really? You'd be interested in that? Hey, I think the sub who's working right now might like some help. Maybe he could teach you some tricks of the trade."

"Wow. That would be awesome, Miss Val!" Then Jack remembers his lack of a vehicle. "But how would I get there?"

"Hmm, there is that. Maybe you could catch the bus that comes down Old Stagecoach after school. Then one of us, or the subcontractor, could take you home. Would you be able to do two or three afternoons a week?"

"Yeah! I'm excited. I've been kind of interested in alternative things for a while now."

"I'd say so. For one, you're a male ballet dancer in a small town. Besides going for alternatives, you've got guts. And I absolutely applaud you for that."

By the time Jack leaves the studio on his bike, he feels like a weight has been lifted from his shoulders. Getting rid of his car *and* his job at Dad's auto shop has opened a window of opportunity for something new. Something to get him out of this rut and looking forward.

6

THINGS TO LOOK
FORWARD TO

Julie

*Be in the present, but also
practice for the future.*

The early March days hold promise for Julie. She's looking forward to going to the mall and purchasing her first pair of *pointe* shoes! And in her newly formed friendship with Sophia, she feels more like a big sister to her than to little Cari. *She still doesn't do much of anything other than cry and keep us awake at night—especially poor Mom.*

After school, Sophia's mother picks up the two of them and drives toward the Dance Centre. The four young boys in the back of the van argue noisily and Ms. Hernandez talks louder.

"How was your day, girls? Did you learn anything new?"

"Not really," Sophia answers. "Have you heard any more about *Abuela*?"

Julie listens thoughtfully as the two converse about Sophia's sick grandmother. *How awful that must be for them. It sounds like they're all so close.*

"We probably can't go see her this weekend—probably the next, though." The warm, friendly woman looks both ways and turns left onto Main Street.

"Then can Julie and I go see that movie?"

Julie gets an idea and joins the discussion. "Hey, what if you spend the night at my house on Friday and we go then? I'm sure my mom could take us to the movie and then to ballet the next morning." *At least I hope she can.*

"That's a great idea! Please *Mamá,* may I?" In the passenger seat, Sophia puts her hands together as if praying.

Ms. Hernandez glances over at her daughter, then pulls her attention back to the road. "We'll see. Let me think about it. But it has to be all right with Julie's mom, too."

"Of course! I'll ask her tonight." *Won't that be fun if we get to do this? Since Cari was born, I hardly ever get to go do anything anymore.*

"How's that little sister of yours, Julie? And how's your mother holding up?" Ms. Hernandez shifts her focus from the road ahead, to the rearview mirror, and back again.

"Well, she really makes a lot of noise for such a tiny thing."

"I'm sure that's quite an adjustment—for all of you." She changes lanes and lets the car behind pass. "Are you able to help out much?"

"Yeah—some." Julie pictures Mom's tired face. "Maybe not enough, though."

"I'm sure you all will figure it out. Each new life brings with it an opportunity for growth. Don't you think?"

Sophia laughs. "That must mean we've grown tons then, huh, *Mamá*?"

The three laugh together while the boys squabble in the back.

The two new friends get out of the van and wave goodbye. Brindle meets Sophia at the studio door and hands her a book.

"You left this here on Saturday."

"Oh, so *that's* where it was." Sophia drops her bag onto the floor and takes *To Kill A Mockingbird* from her. "Thanks."

"It's a really good book, by the way. I took it home and reread it over the weekend."

"You read the whole thing already?"

"Yeah—it's *that* good." Brindle smiles and sits down to tie her *pointe* shoes. "The young girl in the story really gets exposed to a lot, as well as her older brother. It's a shame such a beautiful place as the South was *so* prejudiced."

Paige joins in with, "It still is—from what I gather. But my favorite part was about Boo Radley. They were all *so* afraid of him for such a long time."

"And they'd never even seen him, had they?" Brindle furrows her dark, bushy eyebrows.

"It just goes to show—" Paige answers. "People are always so fearful about what they don't know."

Julie settles down next to Brindle and stares at her toe shoes, enviously. "Your mom said I can get mine now. I'm so excited!"

"You didn't tell me. That's *very* exciting." Sophia pushes Julie's shoulder in jest. "And I thought we were friends," she says, smiling.

Julie defends herself. "I'm so sorry, but I was hoping you could come with me. You know, help me pick the right kind?"

Sophia grins. "Maybe—"

Miss Val calls the class to the *barre* and the girls scramble to finish getting ready.

"Hey, Jack? Are you still coming to help out at our place tomorrow?"

"Yes, ma'am," Jack answers enthusiastically and brings the last *barre* out to the center of the floor.

Todd helps adjust it to the right position and teases, "Yup, our Jack here is turning into a real live lumberjack—learning all things logs." He scooches the base over an inch or so as the girls giggle and Miss Val smiles.

"It *is* a real skill, you know—and he's picking it up quickly."

"Thanks. I'm enjoying the work, too."

Julie gathers that Jack must be helping out at Miss Val's place. This "ballet family" she's getting to know involves much more than just dance. It's certainly not what she expected when she'd signed up a year ago. *It's way better.* As the *barre* work continues, she thinks about her current favorite exercise, *ronde de jambe.* But she senses that could change once she starts *pointe.*

Later that evening, Julie asks Mom about taking her and Sophia to the movie on Friday night and then taking them to ballet the next morning.

Mom looks at her as if extremely put out by this. "Really, Julie? Take you guys to the movie *and* pick you up—at night—with an infant in tow. Who do you think I am, anyway, Superwoman?" She puts a hand on her hip. "Well?"

"Well—I don't know." *Why is this so difficult?* "We're really looking forward to it, Mom! Anime movies are *never* in theaters!"

Mom rubs her temples and sighs. "I'm sorry. It's not *your* fault."

"I haven't gotten to do much lately. I thought you'd understand."

"Tell you what—if Sophia's mother can pick you up after the movie and bring you guys back here, I could probably take you to the movie *and* ballet. Find out if that will work, okay?"

Julie pictures this sequence and agrees. "Thanks, Mom. I'll ask."

When Friday night *finally* arrives, Julie is beside herself with anticipation. She's been obsessing about this movie ever since she'd first heard about it. She didn't have anyone to go with until she thought of asking

Sophia. *That girl's got a lot on her plate these days, with her sick grandma and trying to find new friends at the high school. I hope I can be a good friend to her.* Sophia had confided that Deanne now hangs out more with the "cool kids" and Brindle is homeschooling.

"Ready, Mom?" Julie jiggles Cari on her lap, waiting for her mother to take her.

"All set." She takes Cari and Julie puts on her coat.

When they arrive at Sophia's house, Julie runs up the front steps and knocks on the door. Ms. Hernandez answers and Sophia scoots by, giving her mother a peck on the cheek as she leaves.

"*¡Adiós, Mamá!*"

The girls hurry down to the car to embark on their overnight adventure, chanting, "*Life and Hiccup, Life and Hiccup—*"

Cari starts humming along with them, at least that's what it seems like, and Sophia leans over and tickles her. The baby giggles and reaches toward Sophia, and the tickling starts again.

"She's *so* cute, Julie." Sophia smiles and wiggles her finger at Cari, which prompts more grinning and giggling. "You're so lucky to have such a fun little sister. I'll trade you for one of my brothers," she teases.

Mom laughs. "Thanks, but we're kind of fond of this one. Right, honey?"

Julie nods and wonders if her friend is just naturally good with little kids or if she got that way from having so many younger siblings. Either way, she seems to really enjoy being with them. *Maybe I should take lessons from her.*

〜◎〜

The movie theater is packed and Julie's glad they arrived in time to still get seats—and popcorn. Some kids are dressed as their favorite anime characters and Julie almost wishes she'd thought of doing that. *But which one would I be?* They see two seats in the center of one of the middle rows and squeeze by the other patrons and get seated. Almost immediately the theater darkens and the previews begin.

Sophia leans over and whispers, "Would you like this?" She hands her a chocolate bar.

"Where'd you get it?"

"I brought us each one, from home."

Julie grins and takes it from her. "Thanks."

Life and Hiccup begins with two characters sleeping under a tree. As a huge moon rises, the tree shimmers and dances to the exotic and engaging tune. The brightness increases until the entire screen whites out. Low booms can be heard, as if from underneath the seats, increasing in volume. Then a blast in the music jars them, and the most amazing swirling patterns take over, as if from behind the dozing figures beneath the tree.

The movie continues to bombard their senses and they remain riveted. Over an hour later, Julie's body feels like she was actually one of the characters and had gone through all those hair-raising, wild adventures herself. She turns to Sophia. "Wow!"

Sophia sits wide-eyed, looking over. "Wow is right. That was amazing."

This was definitely an experience Julie will be thinking about and processing for days. "I think it's the best movie I've ever seen."

⌇⌇⌇

Back at the house, Sophia nestles into her bedroll on the floor while Julie adjusts her pillows to sit up in bed.

"I don't think I'd want to live the life of Hiccup, would you?" Sophia asks.

Julie reflects back on one scene in particular. "I don't know. Probably not, but what about when she swooped down to the top of the tree and rescued that squirrel? Remember how it made her feel?"

"Oh yeah." Sophia flips over to prop up on her stomach. "But I would have been so scared."

"Well, of course. But she succeeded. What a rush that must have been for her."

"Yeah, I guess."

Julie reaches over to turn off the lamp.

"Hey, Julie?"

"Hmm?"

"Have you watched many other movies like that? I mean—like—super intense cartoons?"

Julie laughs. "I hadn't thought of them like that. Not many movies—more like animated series. And yeah, I suppose. And more lately, since my mom had the baby."

Sophia yawns. "I haven't. I watch a few shows, but if I spend too much time watching stuff, *mi madre* makes me help her in the kitchen or entertain my little brothers. Our house is pretty noisy, and busy. Anyway, I'm sleepy." She yawns again. "Good night."

"Good night." Julie lies awake thinking about how lonely she feels compared to how Sophia must be. *I might like being part of a bigger family. But then again, I wouldn't have as much free time as I do. I'm just glad I had someone to see the movie with me tonight. It was fantastic.*

7

PIROUETTE

Jack

Let dance happen anywhere it strikes.

The weather in mid-March has been unpredictable. This afternoon, puffy white clouds float overhead and the sun warms Jack's back as he carries a stack of pine tongue and groove boards from Miss Val's truck to the house. He's been helping out for a couple weeks now and sometimes they'll even work on Sundays, like today. He skillfully navigates his way through the open doorway, careful not to bump anything on either end, and then places them neatly on top of the others.

"Is that all of 'em?" Sam asks, climbing down the ladder with power drill in hand. He's the main subcontractor who's doing this part of the interior work.

"Yup," Jack responds. And he adds, since he figures he'll be asked anyway, "and I can stay as late as you need me today. Oh—" Jack turns toward him. "Can I get a ride home from you later?"

"Yeah, that'll be fine. It'll probably be around four."

The two of them are currently trimming out the windows and Jack finds he's really enjoying learning how to do this. But he also has to do the majority of the cleanup work, and there's a lot. Construction is messy and he's constantly sweeping sawdust and debris into an oversized dustpan, and emptying it into a large plastic trash can before dumping it into the dumpster outside. Anything that might be long enough to be useful later is put into the wood stack, and the "crap wood," as Miss Val refers to it, is carried to a different pile for firewood—for their future wood-burning stove.

Jack holds up a partially used tube of adhesive. "Hey, Sam—where do you want this?"

He nods toward the chop saw in the corner. "Over yonder."

When Jack returns from his last trip to the dumpster, Sam motions him over. The older man has four nails sticking out of his mouth and he drives each of them into the wall before being able to say anything except grunt.

Finally, his mouth is clear and he hands Jack the measuring tape. "Look here, now. As I've said before, alternative construction takes longer than regular work and we have to be extra careful so we don't mess up and have more waste. Measure from the top up there." He points to the upper edge of the window opening. "All the way down to the bottom."

Jack does as instructed. "Like this?"

"Mm hmm. How long is it?"

He reads the numbers and counts the in-between lines. "Forty-six and seven-sixteenths."

"Okay, then. For a board to go along this side, what needs to happen from here to there?" Sam runs his finger along the entire length.

Jack studies the curve of the logs next to the straight-edge plank. "Notch it where the logs stick out?"

"Pretty much." Sam steps back and rubs his scruffy chin. "We'll have to scribe the board to match the curve of each log."

"Huh." Now Jack steps back and stares at the area in question. "And how do we do that?"

"We make a template and then draw around it on the board so we can then cut it exactly right." And to clarify, Sam says, "Out of cardboard."

"Oh, that sounds complicated."

"It is. Most contractors around here have no clue how to do that. But I do and I'm gonna teach you." Sam's eyes twinkle when he turns around and grins. "But we'll do that another day. By the way, Val tells me you're a pretty good dancer. Ballet, right?"

Jack nods, unsure of where this is leading.

Sam leans against the window sill and crosses his arms over his barrel chest. "Don't tell anyone, but I used to take line dancin' class. I was never any good at it, though. I was wonderin'—could you show me a turn, or somethin'?"

"What—like a *pirouette*?"

Sam claps his hands once, then motions to the middle of the room. "Yeah, a *pirouette*, that's it. Do one of those, okay?"

Jack sheepishly grins and works up his nerve. "Here?"

"Yeah, out in the middle there."

"O-k-a-y—" Jack walks over, as deliberately as he can, and opens his hands by his sides. "Here?"

"Yup. You ready?"

There, on the sawdust-covered, plywood floor, Jack centers himself and decides to spot Sam's face. *This is ridiculous. Ballet in dirty jeans and a t-shirt. And boots?* He tries to visualize his pants being tights. *Ha!* But then he thinks of this week's Dancespiration: *Let dance happen anywhere it strikes.* He laughs at the synchronicity of this. "Okay, here goes."

Slowly, Jack opens his arms *en a la seconde* and *tendus* to his left side. After bringing his left foot behind, he *pliés* in fourth position to prepare. Then on his own internal clock, he *relevés* onto his right leg, pressing down into the floor as Miss Val has taught him to do, and picks up his back leg into the *passé* position. As if in slow motion, he counts the revolutions he makes by the number of times Sam's face flashes by his focus: one, two, three, four. *Wait—was that actually a quadruple turn? I've never done that before!* Jack ends in a deep lunge with his heart pounding.

Sam claps loudly, the sound echoing in the cavernous room. "Well done, my boy. Well done!"

Another round of applause comes from the doorway, where Miss Val is standing. "Good job, Jack! I'll have to include that in your choreography now, won't I?"

Jack can hardly believe it. "The most I've ever been able to do before was a triple, and it's not even that often!" His hands drift up behind his head and he can't help but smile. "I can't believe I just did that!"

Miss Val laughs. "Sometimes all it takes is a dirty construction site to inspire us, eh?"

The laughter spreads and finally Sam says, "All right, all right. Time to get back to work."

The afternoon passes quickly and Jack remains in a super good mood. He's enjoying this new feeling of lightness and a kind of shift in his quality of life. *I'm not sure what this is, but I kinda like it.*

By Tuesday's ballet class, Jack is feeling a little more on top of his parts in *Coppélia*. When he partners with Randi, their movements flow and he can pretty much anticipate things. But with Deanne, he has to stay on his toes. She does have a history of just looking out for number one—herself. *It's like she's in her own world and just expects me to be there. It's exhausting. And she's kind of full-of-herself. But—I have danced with Randi a lot longer.*

Miss Val instructs Jack and Deanne to try their *pas de deux* full-out with music. They've just marked through it with no music and ironed out a couple rough spots in the choreography.

The notes begin and Franz sneaks up to Coppélia sitting on the chair—in straight and rigid doll form. He waves—nothing. He blows kisses—she still stares at the open book she holds. Jack then goes around behind and taps her shoulder. She turns her head abruptly. He jumps back, as if surprised.

Gently, he coaxes her into standing, then kneels, bringing his hands to his heart. Deanne begins to dance in broken, fragmented movements and Jack closes in to partner with her. He grasps her hips from behind as she pitches downward into a *penché arabesque* and then jerks upright much faster than usual. Jack loses his grip and has to re-grab her in an unfortunate, undignified manner to keep them both from falling on the floor.

"Hey, watch your hands, buddy!" Deanne yelps, but she's laughing.

"Deanne, give the poor guy a break, will you?" Miss Val calls from the corner. "You guys have to work *together*, and *feel*, intuitively, where the other is. You know—try to be in sync?"

"I was." She smirks.

"Mm hmm," Jack responds, mocking her self-righteousness.

Miss Val stops the music and has them practice the sequence with more predictable timing. It's improving and she tells them to commit it to muscle memory. She talks about this a lot, and also insists on the importance of a backup plan, in case you can't remember the choreography.

After the piece is practiced again, the class is instructed to go over their own parts while she works with Franz and Swanilda.

"And Deanne—why don't you run through your part again, by yourself, okay? Get that timing down."

Jack and Randi gravitate to the center and assume their starting pose: standing in *B-plus*, holding crisscross arms and staring into each other's eyes, as a couple in love. The beautiful notes of the symphony fill the studio and they begin their *pas de deux*. Slow and focused at first with loving gestures: a supported *penché arabesque*; he kneels down and she lays over his shoulder; then he stands for a regal walk around in a small circle, holding her up high; *piqué turns*, each opening into a *developpé*.

As the tempo increases, they execute *cabrioles, grand jetés, brisés,* and *tour jetés*. Randi soars higher with each step: *sauté, tombé, glissade, saut de chat*. After completing that, Jack runs after her to the upstage right corner to make their next pass.

Standing in *B-plus*, behind his partner, Jack momentarily catches his breath. He follows her lead and opens his arms in a simple *port-de-bras*. Then he carefully grips her hips for the assists. Randi jumps high in the *cabriole* so he doesn't have to do much, other than make sure he stays in the right place relative to her. The *tombé* and *glissade* are just traveling steps to propel them forward. Then suddenly, Randi takes off on the wrong foot for the *grand pas de chat* and it's all he can do to keep from pulling her over. His momentum continues forward while hers goes straight up.

I gotta let go! He does, then falls sideways across the diagonal while she manages to catch herself in a very un-ballerina-like, Sumo wrestler-looking squat. Jack slides on his left hip and shoulder, but at least he doesn't take her down with him.

Miss Val stops the music. "Are you two all right?"

Jack sits up, a little stunned, and rubs his arm. "Feels like it."

Randi stands over him and offers a hand up. "I'm so sorry! I forgot and picked up the wrong foot for the *pas de chat.*"

He reaches up to take her hand. *She's so sweet. I might just kind of like her.* He manages a "thanks" and grins nervously.

Randi gives him a quick squeeze on the arm.

Does she like me, too? Oh, but what about Todd? Then he remembers they broke up last fall. They weren't super serious anyway. *What's wrong with me—thinking about all this right now?* He shakes his head and says, "Shall we try it again, Miss Val?"

"Are you guys up for it?"

Randi smiles and looks at Jack, raising her eyebrows. "I guess we are."

They run through that particular series again, with no mishaps, and then start the variation again. Jack concentrates on each step his partner makes, trying to be more in tune with her movements. This time, the *pas de deux* goes smoothly and he grows increasingly aware of Randi's proximity. *Her sweat even smells good.* He's having to concentrate much harder than usual to keep his focus from wandering. *Come on, pull it together, man*. He tells himself this over and over while using muscle memory to remember the dance.

By the time class is over, Jack's head is swimming. *Did I hit my skull on the floor? I don't think so.* Miss Val dismisses the class and Randi goes to the door to let in the Beginners. She's been assisting with the other classes for a long time. Jack grabs his things and waves to her, sheepishly, as he heads for his bike. *Maybe the fresh air will clear my mind.*

8

NEW POINTE SHOES!

Julie

No pain, no gain?

A light rain is falling outside, dimming the natural light coming in through the large studio windows. After they finish the *grand battements*, Julie and Sophia carry their *barre* over to the side wall. Miss Val tells them to quickly stretch so they can begin rehearsing.

Julie enviously watches Sophia remove her *pointe* shoes, beyond ecstatic for this afternoon. "I can't wait to get mine—today!" She wiggles her knees up and down, doing butterfly and tipping her head side-to-side.

"You're going to get your toe shoes today?" Randi asks as she screws the cap back onto her water bottle. "How exciting!"

"Mm hmm."

"'Scuse me, Randi," Jack says, lifting the *barre* over as she ducks. He then walks over to the far corner to wipe his feet in the rosin.

Paige stands up and bends over, stretching her hamstrings. "Who's going to the ballet in San Diego next month?"

"We are, of course," Brindle answers. "At least my mom, Willow, and I are."

Deanne lunges into her left leg and then slides down into the splits. "Me, too. I've always wanted to see *The Twelve Dancing Princesses.*"

"Have the rides been figured out yet? I know I'll need one if I'm going to be able to go." *I wonder if I'm the only one who's never been to a professional ballet performance before.* Julie imagines herself there—*an evening at "The Ballet."*

Annie says she's going to try to go, but isn't sure yet.

Miss Val looks up from her choreography notebook. "Let's start with the dance in the toy shop. We need Swanilda and her friends."

Julie follows Randi and the other girls out to the center. The teacher points out where the various life-size toys will be so they'll know where to interact with them, since they won't practice with those dancers until full rehearsals begin in May. This isn't the first time she's gone over this, but Miss Val is a conscientious teacher who wants to make sure everyone is as clear as possible. She places the small trash can, her desk chair, the stool, a box of tissue, and Brindle's sweatshirt around the stage to mark the places where the dancers, dressed as toys, will be.

"Who's the trash can, Miss Val?" Todd asks, chuckling.

She looks down at her notes. "The doll with the trashcan lid balanced on her head."

"Hey, how come nobody gets to be toilet paper?"

Through the laughter, Annie scrutinizes Todd while smiling. "Do you always have to be so—silly?"

"Yes, always."

"Okay, everybody, let's pull it together," Miss Val says with a grin and shake of her head. "We have a lot to do today."

Julie really likes this dance. It's fun and has the potential of being really funny to the audience. That's why they go over it in such detail and soon, hopefully, they'll know the number well enough to be able to relax and bring their own personalities into it. That's when it really gets enjoyable.

They begin by walking through the dance without music, following Randi on from stage left. They are sneaking into Dr. Copelius' toy shop, following Swanilda, who holds a giant key. The toymaker had dropped it in the street out front. Swanilda wants to find the girl who sits in the window and flirts with her *fiancé*, Franz. And, of course, her friends insist on joining her.

While the girls wander through the maze of dolls, Randi exits stage right and immediately returns, dragging a chair with Deanne sitting stiffly in it, holding a book. Once in place, Swanilda spins Coppélia around playfully, but is rather perturbed when the girl doesn't respond. Randi snatches the book away from her and skips around the toys, pretending to read. Julie and the others stand downstage left, watching the interaction attentively.

When nothing happens, Swanilda cautiously goes back to Coppélia and waves her hand in front of her face, trying to get her attention. When that doesn't work, she goes around behind and discovers the wind-up key in her back. She points this out to her friends and they laugh. Swanilda winds up the mechanical doll and watches her dance into the group of toys as they all come to life.

At the end of the piece, Deanne collapses on the floor and it is here that the trashcan lid will fall off the one toy's head and clatter to the floor. Annie pretends to faint and the others catch her. Randi then runs around to each object and mimes winding them up. When the next tune begins, they'll all come back to life.

Now the girls join in the dance, mocking their motions and having a good time. The movements become quite animated even though all the toys are only dancing in place. Swanilda and her friends mimic the gestures of the toys around them and poke fun at what they've discovered.

When the dancers practice it with music, Julie notices how much more real it feels, even though the toy characters are just props at this point. It's like she's actually with this group of friends, way back when, and they've broken into the shop above Main Street and are playing with Raggedy Ann and Andy, and other make-believe novelties. The girls giggle through the dance and, once again, she is reminded how lucky she is to be taking classes at the Dance Centre, *Home of the story ballet*. That's its motto.

The rehearsal progresses and Miss Val steps in to do the mayor's role in Act One, offering the young couple a bag of money for their upcoming nuptials. At first, it was thought Annie would be able to play both roles, friend and mayor, but it became clear that would not be possible. She had been relieved, since as everyone knows, she's rather busy with her college classes and modeling gigs. Annie is a beautiful, exotic-looking Asian-American who's quite talented. Everything seems easy for her.

Miss Val calls the end to rehearsal and Julie joins Sophia as they gather their things to leave together.

"Bye, Deanne! Bye, Brindle," Sophia says, waving back through the doorway.

"See you," Brindle answers.

Randi calls out to them, "Have fun getting toe shoes today! Hey—and welcome to our *pointe* shoe club!"

They laugh together.

"Thanks," Julie responds and follows Sophia out to the parking lot.

"Thank you so much for taking me today, Ms. Hernandez. I don't know when I'd have been able to get *pointe* shoes if my mom had to take me," Julie says, climbing into the minivan and fastening her seatbelt.

"It's no trouble, Julie. It's not often we get a girl's afternoon out, is it, Sophia?"

"That's for sure. I'm so excited." Sophia turns around from the front passenger seat and bounces happily from side to side as her mother backs away from the curb in front of the studio. "I'm starving. Are you?"

"Yeah, kinda—" Julie realizes she hasn't eaten since breakfast, and the rehearsal after ballet class lasted until noon.

"Can we go through a drive-through, *Mamá*? Before we leave Nuevo? I'd love a burger and fries."

"Okay, I suppose we can." Ms. Hernandez smiles and turns left onto Main, instead of turning right to head down to San Diego.

Julie orders a chicken burger and offers a five-dollar bill, but Sophia's mom declines it, saying it's her treat.

She's such a nice lady. "Thank you so much. I'm super glad we get to do this today."

They eat their lunch on the drive and Julie notices how good her food tastes. *Maybe it's the good company, or the excitement of getting toe shoes for the first time.* "Hey—how's your grandmother doing? Is she feeling any better?"

Sophia sadly looks toward her mother before turning around. "Not too well. She's going through chemotherapy now and it makes her really sick."

Ms. Hernandez adds, "I wish we were able to spend time with her more often, but that border crossing is a nightmare."

"But we're going next weekend, right, *Mamá*?"

"Yes, but it's already been three weeks."

"I remember when I was younger, we went down to Ensenada a couple times. It didn't seem like we had to wait very long then."

"It's gotten a lot worse lately—especially with all the bad politics and increased security—particularly if you *look* Mexican. Don't get me started."

Julie tries to think of something she can contribute to the conversation and remembers the latest topic in her history class. "Immigration policies have also changed quite a bit, at least according to my social studies teacher. Is that right?"

Sophia wipes her mouth with a napkin and wads up the burger wrapper. "*Mi papá* says it's gotten really hard, even for people who have lived in the U.S. for a long time, like twenty years, and have paid taxes the whole time. *Es muy difícil, eh Mamá?* Sorry, Julie, I can't help it. Sometimes I just slip into Spanish."

Julie smiles. "Oh, don't apologize. I just wish I understood more."

The conversation jumps from immigration and Mexican hospitals to classes at school. Ms. Hernandez pulls into one of the large mall parking lots and the girls get out, agreeing to meet her in front of the Apple store in two hours.

Sophia pulls her handbag over her shoulder. "That should give us plenty of time. Don't you think?"

"I would hope so." Julie nods and then waves back as she closes the car door. "To the dancewear shop first, right?"

"You bet. *Mamá* said I could get a new pair, too, so I'll have time to break them in before the performances."

Once inside, they step off the escalator onto the second floor and Julie looks up at the huge skylights in the ceiling and points. "Hey look. It's raining again."

Sophia squints upward. "Oh yeah, it is. But it's not going to rain on our parade, though, is it?"

Julie smiles. "Nope, it sure isn't."

They walk down the long aisle and turn into the store, then head straight to the pink satin beauties on the back wall.

Sophia starts at one end and inhales all the way to the other. "That's what Randi does." She starts laughing.

"What? I don't get it."

"No way! You don't know?"

"Know what? Randi sniffs like a dog?"

Now they're both laughing.

"No—Randi *loves* the smell of new *pointe* shoes. She's practically rabid about it."

"Really? I never knew that." Julie stands there, staring at the glossy sheen of the lineup, and tries to picture Randi doing that.

"May I help you ladies?" asks the young clerk, walking toward them.

They both turn and Julie says, "Yes, please. I'm here to get my very first pair of toe shoes." She rubs her palms together nervously.

"How exciting!" She looks at Sophia. "And are you here for moral support?"

"Yeah, kind of. But I need a new pair, too, since mine are wearing out." She tells her the size and brand, and the woman disappears through a curtained doorway.

"What kind do you think I should get?" *There are so many brands.*

"We should ask the lady. That's what she's here for." Sophia takes the box from the clerk when she reappears and goes to a bench to try them on.

"So, what size street shoe do you wear and are your feet wide or narrow?"

After Julie tells her the size and that her feet are not wide at all, the lady shows her a few brands. She picks one and when Julie tries them on, the shoes really pinch her toes.

"They're never very comfortable. You just need to find the ones that are the least *un*comfortable." Sophia hobbles over to join them, waddling like a stiff duck.

"Why are you walking like that, and aren't they supposed to have ribbons on them?"

"Not yet. You have to sew them on after you buy them, silly." Sophia plods back to the bench.

"Oh yeah—Miss Val did say something about that." She pulls off the offending appendage and asks to try a different brand. "And maybe a slightly bigger size, too?"

"Of course." The lady hands her another pair and Julie joins Sophia on the bench.

After three more styles of *pointe* shoes, Julie thinks she's finally found the ones that hurt the least. "I guess I'll take these." She wraps the pretty pink shoes with the tissues and tucks them neatly back into the box.

"All right, then. Would you like wide or narrow ribbons with these?"

Julie looks over at Sophia and stares back at the clerk.

"Perhaps wide would be best, especially since you're just starting out."

Julie nods. *There's so much to know. I would never have been able to figure this out on my own.* "I'm really glad you brought me, Sophia. If I'd have come with my mom and the baby—I don't know if I would've survived."

The clerk smiles and rings them up. "It does get easier."

Sophia glances at her phone as they leave the store. "Just enough time to window shop on all three floors before we have to meet my mom. You game?"

"Yes. It was intense in there, but so awesome!" Julie grabs Sophia by the arm and they pass by displays of musical instruments, camping equipment, and attire for seemingly *every* occasion. They finally reach the Apple store and Ms. Hernandez is there to greet them. It's been an absolutely fantastic day and Julie can't wait to get home and show off her new *pointe* shoes to Mom.

9

CAUSE AND EFFECT

Jack

Keep your eye on the target, whether spotting in a turn or rehearsing a part.

By the end of March, the days finally feel longer, with more daylight hours in the afternoons. Jack has recently become interested in the nuances of the natural world around him—things like the effects of the spring equinox, the first day of spring, and how it seems to bring with it a kind of hopefulness in the plant and animal kingdoms. Flowers begin to bloom, baby animals are born, even people come across as more hopeful. But perhaps he and his fellow students are just seeing the light at the end of the tunnel as the last day of school slides into view.

Miss Val instructs the class to stretch and get ready for rehearsal. The *barre* exercises were moderate today as more and more of their class time needs to be spent learning and practicing their parts for *Coppélia*.

"Hey, Jack, are you going to the ballet with us?" Deanne asks.

Jack leans into a right lunge. "I'm not sure yet. Is it during spring break?"

Randi scrolls through her phone and finds what she's looking for. "Nope, it's after."

Miss Val looks up from her notebook. "Well, we all have to decide pretty soon, while we can still get a group rate. And remember, it's for the Sunday matinée."

"I'm going. And Brindle and Sophia and Randi and Paige—you are, right?" Deanne asks.

They all nod back at her.

"And, hopefully, I can go, too," Julie adds.

"Great." Miss Val smiles and turns back toward the stereo. "Okay—let's begin with the first villager dance, shall we?"

"Hey, Jack." Randi taps his shoulder. "I signed up for that ballet master class in San Diego. You know, the one Miss Val mentioned a while back? I think you should, too."

He turns to face her as they walk out to the center of the floor. "Oh yeah—I probably will. Thanks for reminding me."

Jack takes Randi's hands in his and the couple stands in center stage. The music begins to play, in stately 4/4 time, and they smile, gazing into each other's eyes. As townsfolks, Paige, Annie, Brindle, Sophia and Julie move into formation around them. Jack prepares for his supporting role along with the *cabrioles, pas de chats, pas de basques,* and *tour jetés.* The music begins;

the dancers fill the studio with lively movement and Jack falls into his role as Franz.

Assisting his partner upward in her *assemblé battu*, Jack holds her up a tiny bit longer so she can finish the beat and close in fifth. He feels the warmth of her sides. *Slightly moist from sweating at the barre, most likely.* It makes for a better grip so he can lift her higher. The next phrase includes a *cambré* back in *soussus,* where she leans back over his shoulder. She accidentally turns her face toward him, and giggles, as it's obviously wrong. The air escaping her lips tickles his ear and he snickers, too. *This sure feels good—her being this close.*

After she pulls up off his shoulder, he prepares himself for the supporting role in her *arabesque promenade.* He moves into position to walk around her so she can pivot in this lovely ballet pose, but he gets flustered by her proximity and struggles to clear his mind. *Come on now, get your head together,* he tells himself. *Do I really like her?*

The next few bars go smoothly and Miss Val calls out minor instructions to the group as they continue the piece. "Brindle, link your other arm with Sophia's. Don't look at the floor, Paige. Point those feet, everyone!"

When the dance ends, the next one immediately follows and they roll right into it. Franz exits and Swanilda begins trying to get the attention of Coppélia. She gestures, she dances, and she mocks the girl in the window—all to no avail. After all her unsuccessful attempts, she angrily stomps off stage. They all laugh as Randi performs impromptu gesticulations like sticking her tongue out and blowing a raspberry as she exits, and Deanne does the same, and more, back at her.

Miss Val laughs, too, but adds, "It's all very funny, but you might want to find other humorous gestures that could actually be used onstage. Not you, Deanne. You're a rigid doll. Just you, Randi."

"Yes, just me, you brainless piece of plastic," Randi teases.

Deanne laughs along with the others and then Jack gets ready for his flirtations with Coppélia.

Deanne sits up straight in the chair, holding a book she pretends to read. For now, she makes do with any book that's available, and today it happens to be a dance magazine she'd pulled from the stack on Miss Val's desk. When the music begins, Jack cautiously approaches Deanne and notices the picture on the cover. He can tell it's from the ballet *Giselle,* and he's taken back to his *pas de deux* with Randi in that ballet, and how they barely managed to pull off that scary shoulder sit. But he dismisses these thoughts so he can focus on his current role, *the stupid guy who falls for a doll.*

He waves at her, blows kisses, kneels, and places his hands over his heart pleadingly—all for no returned affection. *Just like a real girlfriend.*

Swanilda wanders onto the stage behind him and watches, in horror, as her beloved Franz flirts mercilessly with that wicked girl in the window. Of course, when he realizes she has seen him, he pantomimes, while dancing, how sorry he is. But she's hurt and keeps pushing him away. Jack and Randi continue their argumentative dance and he can sense actual tension coming from her.

Wow. I'm glad this isn't a real spat. She's on fire.

Swanilda abruptly exits stage left, leaving poor, hapless Franz to dwell in self-pity. *Oh me, oh my, poor me.* Jack can't help but smile at this typical scenario so many of his own gender find themselves in—over and over again.

But then, Coppélia starts blowing kisses to Franz. Jack feigns infatuation with the girl in the window and begins his own *showing off* dance. After each move, he turns to make sure she's still watching. She is, so he continues his grandiose gestures to communicate his new love for her. *What a guy. Deanne is cute. Oh, man, am I this shallow, too?* Jack continues to the end of the piece and it's clear the whole class has gotten wrapped up in it. They all applaud at the end and he takes a rather sheepish bow.

"Way to go, Franz!" Todd bellows, which of course is funny coming from him—like everything else he does.

That guy could really be a great comedian. He's got talent, or a knack, or something. Jack turns to the mirror, prepares, and does an almost perfect triple outside *pirouette*.

"Good one, Jack." Miss Val smiles and tells the girls to assemble for the dance where they find Dr. Coppelius' key. "Oh, but first let's do your part, Jack, where you and your little buddies harass Dr. Coppelius, okay?"

Jack nods, and when the first notes flow from the stereo, he walks toward stage right, gesturing encouragingly to his currently invisible friends. Miss Val says there will be two or three from the Intermediate class who will be his sidekicks. And he's hoping he can also talk his friend, Mike, into joining them. After all, he'd convinced him to be Drosselmeyer in *The Nutcracker* last year.

Todd, as Dr. Coppelius, is pretending to lock the door below Coppélia's window, as if in the street. As Franz approaches, he's surprised and gets flustered when Franz pantomimes wanting to be let upstairs to see Coppélia. Of course, the mad scientist does *not* want him to know she's only a doll and refuses. Franz pleads again, but the answer is still no. At this point, Franz gets angry, and with the help of his *imaginary* friends, he starts to tussle with Dr. Coppelius. After the altercation, the old man brushes off his clothes and readjusts his, as yet, nonexistent hat. It's here that he, unknowingly, drops his key in the street and then staggers offstage.

Before long, class is over and the Beginners stream in through the door. Jack hears one of them squeal and ask, "Oh goodie, Miss Val! Do we get to do magazines today?"

She smiles and ushers the girl past her desk so the others can get by. "Maybe, we'll see if there's time." Often, near the end of class, they'll get to do different fun things that pertain to dance like acting out stories, balancing on the wobble board, and freestyle dancing. And perhaps today they'll get to mimic poses from magazine pictures while the class watches. This gives them extra practice for performing in front of an audience.

~⦿~

On Sunday afternoon, Jack finds a place to sit on the rough-finished porch of Miss Val's log cabin. He drops his sack lunch down on the top step. He's worked all morning, since around eight, and it's already one. He removes the baseball cap and shakes his head. Sawdust settles down to the deck and he mops his sweaty brow. The palm sander beats having to sand everything by hand, but it sure is messy. Luckily, he's brought plenty of water and chugs it thirstily—then remembers his can of iced tea, which he'd put in the freezer last night.

Gratefully biting into his salami and cheese sandwich, he leans back into the log column, takes a long swig of tea, and relaxes. A little brown canyon wren hops around nearby like it wants a handout. He pulls a crumb of bread off a corner of the sandwich and rolls it across the porch. The bird scurries to the morsel and quickly flies off with it. There are so many different kinds of birds here. He's been curious about them the last few weeks and Miss Val has mentioned the names of a few.

Jack practically inhales his banana after finishing the two sandwiches. *This construction work sure builds up an appetite. I wish I'd brought more food.* The bird comes hopping back with its now familiar song, so he digs around in the bag for another stray crumb. "Ahh, success, my friend. Here you go." This time he only tosses it a foot away and the little bird ventures closer and retrieves it. "Bye, buddy. I gotta get back to work."

A squirrel chirps repetitively nearby, like a warning signal or a sledgehammer hitting a steel pipe. *Music of the canyon.* The noisy sentinel stands on a boulder up the hill and continues his message while Jack puts new paper on the head of the sander and gets back at it. The little motor in the tool vibrates his hand and he quietly sings to himself. "I don't get paid for doing nothin'." A lizard scrambles across the floor and out the open doorway.

An hour later, he takes a break from the sander and starts putting putty in the holes that were created after sinking tiny nails into the trim boards. It's a quiet and methodical task that allows him to ponder as he works. Dip a finger in the can, smear it into the hole, then clear the excess away with a different finger. A cloth rag hangs from his front pocket so he can periodically clean off his hands. He passes by the large window in the master bedroom and notices two squirrels, not four feet from him, standing on their hind legs picking red berries from the bush outside.

Not wanting to disturb them, he stops and watches. They reach up with their little hands and grab one berry at a time and eat it—gnawing one side before turning it over to analyze and then chewing on the other side. *They look like a little old couple, standing there and picking fruit in an orchard.* Jack slowly shifts his weight to his other foot so he can get a less obstructed view. *This is better than TV. They're still at it; I can't believe it. I wonder how long they've been together?* He thinks back to the role he's dancing, as Franz, and whispers, "I'll bet you guys don't concern yourselves with silly, frivolous things, do you? No, probably not. I'll bet you've got it all figured out— about what's important in life, and all—"

Suddenly, a bigger squirrel races over and steals a berry out of one of their paws and takes off with it.

"You bully! Who do you think you are, anyway?"

Unfortunately, Jack's outburst has scared Mr. and Ms. Squirrel away and he feels bad about it. *Those two squirrels were amicably working and eating together in harmony. Why did that robber come and just steal their berry? He could've easily gotten his own.* With new clarity he's summoned from this vicarious experience, out of the blue he starts thinking about the importance of rules and regulations in society. *Of course, there are still thieves among us. But what would it be like if there was no law of the land? Total anarchy—that's what.* He wonders why these random thoughts just pop into his head sometimes. And this makes him remember that he'd better study for tomorrow's civics test.

Jack hears the truck pull in front of the cabin and in a few minutes Miss Val appears. "How's it going, Jack?"

"Pretty well, I'd say." He points out the sanding and puttying he's finished, and the Australian shepherd bounds in and licks Miss Val's hand.

"It looks good to me. Good boy, Nutkins. Yes, yes, I missed you, too." She kneels down and rubs his face with both hands. "Hopefully, I got everything Sam needs for this week. I spent hours down the hill gathering supplies. I'm glad to finally be home."

She releases the dog and walks through the house inspecting the recent work.

"I hate to ask, but can I get a lift back later?"

"Of course. How about in an hour or so? Let me just put the groceries away and feed all the critters."

On the way home that Sunday evening, Miss Val asks Jack about how his econ class is going.

Jack groans. "I don't know. We've been studying economic growth and how it's crucial to a stable society. But it still rubs me the wrong way."

Miss Val turns off the dirt road onto the paved street and laughs. "I'm sorry. I don't mean to laugh, but sometimes you just have to—you know, to stay sane."

He looks over at her and envies how on top of things she seems. He's tired and just starts talking, off the cuff. "Even if constant growth *was* sustainable, it all feels so shallow to me. We just follow whatever our current infatuations are, like our culture with its nice cars, fancy clothes, and money—but it's never enough."

"And it's not, for a lot of people. Our advertising just promotes that mentality and behavior. And no, it certainly is *not* sustainable."

"Jack turns to face her. "Hey, Miss Val—did you ever read *The Giver?*"

"Yes. What a wonderful book! Why do you ask?"

"I liked it, too. I remember how everyone in the society just went along without questioning anything.

And then Jonas comes along and starts questioning everything."

"Mm hmm, it's what got him into so much trouble, but then ultimately saved everyone in the end, right?"

"Yeah." Jack sits quietly for a moment. "I really liked that guy."

Miss Val glances over. "Me, too."

Their conversation gives him a lot to think about. Like how hard it is to *not* follow our attractions—like poor, hapless Franz in *Coppélia* does— and muddy-brained Jack sometimes when he's around Randi, or Deanne or...

10

SPRING BREAK

Julie

Reward those hard-working, sore muscles with a nice, hot soak in an Epsom salt bath. It feels great!

"You can do it. I know you can!" says the tiny one with short black hair.

Bernie turns around to see who spoke. "Who are you and how do you know who I am?"

Julie gets up from the desk and moves to her bed, staring at the phone screen, and props up a pillow to lean against.

"Hmm, I'm not sure I can tell you that, but I'm here to help you." The character's eyebrows twitch in an odd, unsettling manner.

A giant burning ball drops into the forest, too close for safety, and Julie's heart rate quickens.

"Hurry, come with me!"

Bernie takes a second to think before nodding, and they run, crashing through branches in the opposite direction. The fiery ball chases them deeper into the woods and Julie's breathing matches theirs. She jumps when the lights go out in her room and gasps. The lights come back on and Julie looks toward the door.

"Do you know what time it is?" Mom's leaning on the door frame, yawning.

"It's almost over. I'll go to bed right after this—I promise."

"No, Julie. You'll turn it off right now and go to bed. It's two in the morning and those little tinny voices woke me up."

"It's two already?" *How can that be? I've only watched a few episodes.*

"Yes, and you have school tomorrow." Mom starts to leave, then pauses. "We're going to have to do something about this. It's become a real problem. Give me your phone."

Julie groans, reluctantly turns it off, and slaps it into her mother's open palm. She pulls the covers up around her and pounds the pillow several times, getting it into the right shape. "Get the light?"

"Excuse me? How about a *please?*"

She whispers, "Please—sorry."

The lights go out and Julie is left alone in the dark.

The quad is crawling with kids during lunch today. The weather is perfect and the sun warms Julie's back as she approaches Sophia—who is by herself again.

"Hi, may I join you?"

Sophia squints up and grins. "Yeah, that would be nice."

Julie sits down next to her and pulls out a sandwich. "What did you bring today?"

"PB&J and a fruit cup. What's that, bologna?"

Julie peels the bread back to reveal the contents. "Yup."

"They still sell that stuff? I had no idea." Sophia crinkles her nose.

"Well—" Julie defends. "I like it."

"Whatever floats your boat, I guess."

"Or tickles my fancy."

They snicker at their own cleverness and Sophia nods at the book lying next to her. "I just finished it. And you guys were right. It *is* a good book. Who was it, Paige, who really liked Boo Radley?"

"Yeah, I think it was. But I don't remember a whole lot about *To Kill A Mockingbird*. We just had to read it for English, like you." Julie wraps the crust of her sandwich and puts it back into the bag.

Sophia stares out into the crowd, obviously thinking about something. "I'm super glad I read it. It brings up the same kinds of problems we still have today. People of color really do get a rotten deal—at least about some things."

The bell rings and Julie wants to say something nice. "It isn't fair, that's for sure. Hey, how's your grandma doing?"

Sophia picks up the book and stands. "Hopefully, she's getting near the end of her chemotherapy. Then we'll know more."

"Are you going to see her again soon?"

They start walking toward the lockers and Sophia answers. "I think so. Oh, *mi mamá* says I probably can't go to that ballet because of *mi abuela.* We're going down to Tijuana as often as we can right now."

"That's too bad. But it's good you get to see her, right?"

"Yeah," Sophia says, absentmindedly.

The students are dispersing, heading for their respective classrooms, and the custodians begin their daily task of cleaning up the quad.

✵

After school, Julie is surprised to see Dad in the pickup line. She immediately wonders, *what's wrong?*

"Hi, honey. Did you miss me?"

Even for an airline pilot, he was gone longer than usual this time, and he hardly ever picks her up from school. She gets into the passenger seat and leans over to hug him. "Of course, I did. Is everything okay— Mom, Cari?"

Dad laughs. "Yes, they are. Very well, in fact." He pulls out into the street toward home. "And you will be, too, when you hear the news."

Her stomach flips in anticipation. "Well—are you going to tell me or not?" The dashboard beeps and she remembers to fasten her seatbelt.

"Okay, you ready?" He grins extra big, showing all his teeth.

She nods excitedly. "Mm hmm."

"You know how spring break is next week, right?"

"Y-e-a-h." *Get to the point, Dad.*

"We're going to Puerta Vallarta!"

"Really? That's in Mexico, right?"

"It is."

"Wow! You can get the time off?"

Dad looks at her, raising his eyebrows. "As it turns out, I'm flying there on Monday and am taking the rest of the week off. And you guys are coming with me." He tips his head back into the headrest and grins.

"And Mom's okay with taking Cari?" *This is beginning to sound a little tricky, but also very exciting—and so unexpected.*

"She's all in. Our family could use some quality time together, don't you think?"

"Absolutely," Julie says, trying to wrap her head around this. *A family vacation—out of the blue like this. Who would have thought it would ever be possible?*

That evening, over dinner, they discuss their last-minute plans and make lists of what they need to do before leaving—*in just five days!*

Less than a week has passed since Julie learned about their impromptu vacation. She settles into the window seat and Mom holds Cari in the aisle while Julie fastens the car seat in the center.

"You sure it's tight enough?"

Julie rocks the carrier back and forth. "It seems like it."

Mom straps the baby in. "Away we go. Puerta Vallarta, here we come!"

"Yeah, I can't believe we're really doing this!" Julie looks out the window practically the whole time, since her little sister is taking a nice long nap—the taxi out to the runway, takeoff, flying through the clouds, and finally descent and landing.

Cari wakes up when the pressure changes and cries a little bit, but they've been lucky. The nearly three-hour flight passed quickly and now they're here! As they disembark, she smiles at Dad, who's greeting the exiting patrons.

"Hi Dad."

He tells them to meet him in the luggage pickup; he should be there in a half hour or so.

After the taxi ride from the airport, they check into the hotel, change their clothes, and head down to the pool. Julie throws her towel on a lounge chair and eases down the steps into the amazingly warm water. It's not too crowded, so she swims to the other end and pulls herself out. *Time for sunbathing. I definitely plan to go back home with a tan.* Mom and Dad have taken Cari over to the baby pool.

That evening, at the hotel restaurant, they go over their itinerary for the week: tomorrow, spend most of the day at the beach and maybe walk to the boardwalk that evening; Wednesday, take a bus to the Botanical Gardens; and Thursday, probably visit the Lagoon and maybe do the River Walk. On Friday they fly home. Dad says they have to make some reservations ahead of time, but there should be room for spontaneity as well. Even Cari is in a good mood this evening. *Maybe it's the change in scenery. This place is beautiful, and the beach is right here.* The evening breeze caresses Julie's freshly tanned shoulders and she is really enjoying her mango shrimp.

The breakfast is almost as delicious as dinner was. They'll go down to the beach together and use the hotel chairs and towels provided for the guests.

"And I'm going to work extra hard on my tan today."

Mom laughs. "I'll bet you will."

"You can too, babe," Dad says. "I can take the baby up to the room later for her nap, and you two can get some girl time together."

Mom raises her eyebrows at Julie. "Imagine that."

By evening, they are all a little sunburned, but remain in good spirits. Julie buys a cute, spaghetti-strapped sundress on the boardwalk and the family stops to watch a fire dancer. Julie gasps when his long black hair nearly catches fire after the burning stick lands on his head. They've heard how many mosquitos there are in the jungle areas, so Mom stops at one of the vendors to get a breathable nursing cover for tomorrow. They'll definitely use the bug spray they brought, but Cari will probably need more veiling.

At nine o'clock on Wednesday morning, they catch a bus from the "Romantic Zone" in Puerta Vallarta to the Botanical Gardens. The bus is crowded, but Julie and her mom find seats while Dad has to stand. Mom holds Cari in her lap. The antiquated vehicle lurches into motion and Julie notices Dad grab the back of a seat for balance. Every time the driver stops to let passengers on or off, which is often, the brakes are applied harshly and it sounds like they're grinding.

Julie looks out her side window at the sparkling bay before they turn eastward into the mountains. *Now for the "windy curvies" we heard about.* Julie braces herself as the bus careens around the turns and threatens to crash at every juncture. She starts to get queasy and closes her eyes, hoping they don't all die on this family vacation. The bus continues to make stops for the laborers who use it to get to work. *They have to ride this thing every day?*

Eventually, they arrive at their destination and wobble off the bus, attempting to get their land legs back.

"Do you have any snacks with you, Mom? That bus ride made me a little sick."

"Me, too. Here's a granola bar. Can we share it?"

Dad takes Cari and they walk toward the entrance to pay with however many pesos this place charges. Julie's noticed the bargaining that goes on in Mexico and wonders if the Botanical Gardens does that, too.

"Two hundred pesos each, *por favor*," says the attendant. And Dad hands it over.

The place is stunning. Julie has never before seen so many shades of green. Dad grabs a couple maps from the stand and they proceed, as directed, through different growing zones: coffee, cacao, bananas, papayas, mangos. The cacao beans are huge and Julie wonders if she can buy some candy or something made from it.

The family wanders through the dense foliage and learns this place opened in 2005 and is one of the top ten gardens in North America. These forty-six hectares are protected by *The Friends of Vallarta Botanical Gardens, A.C.* in collaboration with the U.S. Thousands come here each year to see the exotic plants and observe the birds. Mom is free to be entranced with the beauty all around her, since Dad is carrying the baby wrapped in that new mosquito covering. Julie swats absently at an annoying buzzing around her ear.

The lunch on the restaurant terrace is expensive, but very good. Julie orders mango shrimp so she can compare it to the hotel's. "It's a little different, but just as good."

"How about the two of you hike down to the river and I'll take Cari with me and go see the orchids?" Mom suggests.

Dad puts down his napkin. "Are you sure you're okay with that?"

"Mm hmm. She looks about ready for a nap, anyway. I'll just nurse her and then she'll sleep through it."

The hike down the trail is pretty easy. They both have worn their swimsuits underneath their clothes in case they'd get to swim in the Horcones River.

"Last one in's a rotten egg!" Dad yells.

"Oh, no fair. You got a head start!"

He still looks good, for a middle-aged man, and Julie's not embarrassed to be seen with him not wearing a shirt. He strides right into the swimming hole and sinks down to where he's only a neck and head. Julie laughs and gets in with him. Tropical birds carry on all around them and she's struck at what a tropical paradise this actually is. *And I get to be here— away from school, traffic, homework, and strip malls.* This place feels refreshing. She looks down at her arms and notices how much tanner they look.

The hike back out is all uphill and much harder than coming down was. Sweat runs down her forehead and between her shoulder blades. By the time they get back up to the top, they're both breathing hard.

"Can we get something to drink, Dad?"

He smiles and pats her back. "You betcha, honey. And let's go find Mom."

Dad expresses his surprise upon finding out that the bus ride back is cheaper than the one coming. "Just because it's downhill?"

The family waits on the bench in the covered hut for the rattly old vehicle as it smokes and lumbers toward them. The motor misses and stalls and Julie fans the smelly exhaust from in front of her face. Following Mom up the steps, she almost slips on a banana peel. Fortunately, there are very few people aboard and they find ample, if not the cleanest, seating.

Halfway down the mountain, the bus stalls again, but the driver can't restart it. The sun is sinking behind the trees and he says the next bus is the last one, but won't be by for two more hours. He proceeds down the steps and starts tinkering under the hood. The only other passengers are locals and have deboarded and walked away.

"It's too hot to wait in here," Mom says and gets up with Cari.

"Okay," Dad says. "Let's go find some shade. They walk back about a hundred yards and sit down under a grove of trees.

"I'm hungry—and thirsty," Julie says. "That drink wasn't very big." *I wish we were back at the hotel sipping papaya juice or something. Two hours? You've got to be kidding.*

"I don't have anything," Mom says, rummaging through the diaper bag. "I thought we'd be back by now."

Cari starts crying and nothing consoles her. Mom looks as if she's at her wits' end, so Julie offers to walk with the baby. She lifts her over her shoulder, but the screaming continues. Pretty soon, a woman carrying a basket of vegetables walks out from a dirt road and says something in Spanish. Julie shakes her head, not understanding, and the woman signals for her to follow. Julie shakes her head again and turns back toward Mom and Dad.

A short while later the lady returns with a young child of her own and brings a pail of fruit. She holds it out to them and says something in Spanish again.

"*No entiendo,*" Dad says in his limited Spanish.

She extends the pail toward him and gives it a shake. "*Para ustedes.*"

Dad looks to Mom and she shrugs. Taking it from her, he responds and smiles. "*Gracias.*"

The woman hoists her own child onto her hip and disappears again. The papaya and mango are the best Julie's ever had. They're soft and bursting with flavor. Even baby Cari is mesmerized as she sucks on the succulent fruit.

Half an hour later, the woman returns with a basket of what looks like corn husks. "*Más?*" she asks.

Dad stands and approaches her and a teenage boy. "Corn," the boy says.

"Thank you," Dad says and starts digging in his pocket.

The woman puts up her hands and shakes her head. "*Para su familia—está muy importante.*" The two strangers take the empty fruit pail back and turn to go. They wave and smile and trod barefoot, back the way they came.

Mom thanks them and begins unwrapping the roasted ears of corn. "I can't believe she wouldn't take anything. She's so kind."

Julie bites tentatively into the darkened kernels and closes her eyes. *This is sensational. Food this good, hospitality without reward, happy and helpful kids. Is that how Sophia's family is in Mexico? They do seem so close.* As she chews and looks at Mom, Dad, and Cari and the jungle around them, Julie starts to see her own family in a new light. This moment will be what she remembers most about their trip—more than the fancy hotel and touristy beach. She can't remember feeling this profoundly content in a very, very long time.

11

FROM TROLLEY TO MASTER CLASS

Jack

*This old Dancespiration bears repeating:
Push down through the supporting foot in a
pirouette—instead of concentrating on the rise.*

The alarm goes off at O-dark-thirty and Jack rolls over onto his side to hit the snooze button. After a tiny catnap, it rings again. He's got to get up and get ready so he doesn't miss the bus. He and Randi had signed up for the one-day-only variations class during spring break. Randi offered to give him a ride, but since it's all the way down in San Diego, he thought it might be a good opportunity to check out the limited mass transit firsthand.

He quickly downs a bowl of cereal and packs his lunch, which he'd prepared the night before, into his backpack and heads out the door. Luckily, his bike has a headlight and flashing taillight. He pedals down the street as dawn is breaking and the streetlights are beginning to turn off. The song, *Morning Has Broken*, becomes the soundtrack for his short commute to the bus stop. A warm feeling arises when he thinks of how Dad is always whistling that tune. In the town of Nuevo, there is only one bus in the morning and one in the evening, so there's not much room for error if you need to get somewhere without a car.

He locks his bike onto the bars of the rack at the bus stop, and follows the last person on. There aren't many passengers, but a few more board when the bus makes several stops before heading down the hill to the city. Jack stares out the window into the ravine on the right side. *I sure wouldn't want to take a tumble down there.* The driver brakes before each turn, accompanied by a release of air noise and the need to slightly brace oneself. Nobody's talking. *Maybe because it's so early.*

Thirty-five minutes later Jack gets off the bus and quickly walks across the transfer station parking lot. He finds the correct place and waits five minutes before the trolley arrives. This will take him halfway and then he'll catch another line downtown. The last leg meanders through several distinct mini communities of San Diego proper and Jack enjoys watching each of them come to life. But then a very smelly, disheveled man sits down in the seat next to him. Jack smiles, but the guy starts mumbling incoherently, so he turns back to look out the window for the remainder of the ride.

His stop finally comes and he squeezes past the man and exits the trolley car. *I'd better check out that map to make sure I'm in the right place.* Tracing his finger along the lines he looks to the right and decides that's the direction he needs to go. *I hope I'm not late.* Two blocks down, he realizes he's gone the wrong way, so he starts jogging back, holding the straps of his knapsack firmly so it won't bounce so much. Checking his phone while on the go, he sees the class will start in five minutes! Up ahead on the left, he finally sees the sign for the studio and picks up his pace.

A woman checks him in at the door and points where to go. He drops his backpack along the wall, scans all the dancers' backs spread before him, and finds a spot behind them. Warmups have already begun. The class moves right into *ronde de jambes* and Jack follows along the best he can, without having seen the instruction. As the exercises progress, they become more and more challenging. When *pirouettes* are incorporated, Jack notices several of the dancers doing triples regularly. *Man, they're good. Who do I think I am, anyway?* This throws him off his game for several minutes.

I can do this; I've done it before. I'll just spot the back of that girl's head. Even though some of them are doing the preparation for the turn in a lunge, Jack bends both knees and *pliés* in fourth. *Single, double… quick save. Why won't my triple work today?* The girl who's head he's been spotting turns around. *It's Randi!* He smiles and gets back to focusing—just in time for the Russian teacher to signal them to stretch.

"You made it! I didn't see you when we started." Randi gets her water and drinks thirstily.

"Yeah, I was a little late. But I think I only missed a couple exercises."

The two settle down onto the floor and reach over each leg before sliding into the splits. Jack almost has his right side, but the left is more problematic. He's working on them, though.

Randi leans over and whispers, "I love his accent, don't you?"

Jack nods. "Yeah—but I don't completely understand all his words."

"Enough though, right? At least the ballet terms are familiar."

He nods as the ballet master speaks, and all the dancers return to the floor ready to learn the first variation. When the music begins, his ballerina assistant, who's beyond amazing, demonstrates the beginning. Her lithe body executes each *piqué, pirouette, brisé,* and *fouetté* seamlessly. *She doesn't even look real.*

"Okay, everybody—any questions?" The master puts his arms out and shrugs, but doesn't give enough time for anyone to answer, or ask. "This half go first." He slices down the middle of the room with his arm and scoops it to the side, to get them to move off the floor, while nodding to those chosen for group one.

Jack and Randi glance at each other and breathe a sigh of relief. *At least we get to watch first and have more time to memorize the segment.*

When the music begins, the assistant dances in front as the master points out and dictates the steps. Jack only understands every other word or so, but dutifully marks through the steps, using as little space as possible in the crowded room. During the outside *pirouettes,* there are a couple of dancers who nail both triples, but then they have to scramble to catch up with the music—since extra turns take more time.

At the end, the dancing group is breathing hard and quickly moves off to the sides so the next group can begin. Jack and Randi go to the middle of the pack and the music starts. He remembers the first couple phrases, but then has to watch and copy the ones in front for the next series of steps.

As the *pirouette* sequence approaches, Jack attempts to gain a little extra space for himself by traveling large in the *pas de bourreé* and extending his arms. He *pliés* evenly in fourth position before forcefully pressing down onto his right leg and bringing his left into *passé*. Spotting once, twice, and stopping with the third, he tips off balance and catches himself in a sideways lunge. *At least I didn't fall down—that's happened before.*

The next few steps are a no-go for Jack since the three turns and the fallout took extra time. He skips forward to the turn on the other side—to catch up with the group. He only goes for a double now since this is his weaker side. It's more successful, but he knows he's here to push himself—beyond those self-imposed comfort barriers.

Later, the group is instructed in an *allegro* (fast) pattern. This time there are two groups of girls and one guy group. When the boys are up, the master shouts, "More beats! We stay up in the air longer and you must make it count! Not just *battu*! At least *entrechat seis*!"

Before realizing it, Jack is swept up in the mass of male energy and finds himself powering through the air with more beats to his jumps than ever. The group impetus is palpable and carries him through the routine with a newfound exuberance. When the piece ends, they all walk around in circles, panting heavily.

"Wow, Jack," Randi says as he joins her in back. "That was amazing."

He smiles big. "It felt really good, too."

"Now we learn part of a variation from *Swan Lake,*" the master says in his thick Russian accent. "Let us prepare."

He excuses "the fellows" while he works with the girls. Jack practices his triple turns in a back corner while Randi learns part of Odette's solo, *en masse* with the other "swans." There's a whole lot of *pointe* work involved and Jack's relieved to be able to focus more on sailing through the air—*with the greatest of ease.* He laughs at the thought and a couple guys turn to look at him. He grins back, a little embarrassed, and decides to stretch for a while.

Eventually, the fellows get their turn and are instructed in a portion of Prince Siegfried's solo. There are *cabrioles, grand jetés,* switch leaps, barrel turns, and triple *pirouettes.* Jack can't remember the last time he felt this alive. He's on cloud nine dancing this way, in a group of guys, and he's not even all that focused on the choreography. The movement is what's carrying him, the dance itself. *Can I just live here forever—in this state of bliss?*

He senses Mom answering the question. *Yes and no—but try to embrace the feeling. It can help buoy you when things get challenging.*

Huh? He goes for an impromptu triple and ends in an off-kilter lunge. He grins anyway, and believes Mom wants him to keep dancing. *It's where my passion lies—and my therapy.*

The groups continue to take turns, girls-girls-boys, girls-girls-boys. And since nothing lasts forever, this, too, comes to an end. The class applauds the master and the assistant curtsies. A few of the students mingle, while others grab their things and exit. Randi finds Jack and they sit down in the back, rehydrate, and get ready to leave.

"That was *so* amazing, wasn't it?" Jack says.

"It absolutely was. I can't believe we're the only ones here from Nuevo."

"I know, right? They do *not* know what they missed."

"Hey, do you want a ride back up the hill?"

Jack doesn't want this energy from the class to dissipate so he decides to accept the ride and continue sharing their enthusiasm. "The bus back up to Nuevo doesn't leave until 5:30, anyway. So, thanks."

They make their way to Randi's car, which is four blocks away.

"Wow. That's the closest spot you could find?"

"Yes. It's a good thing I left early enough this morning."

They walk by an old man, sleeping in a corner behind a trash bin, and hurry toward the green light at an intersection. The electronic voice finishes its countdown as they run to the other side. By the time they reach the car it starts to sprinkle.

"Just in time," Randi says, unlocking her door.

Jack puts his bag in the back and settles into the passenger seat and buckles up.

Randi starts the car and rubs her palms together. "Heater?"

"Sure."

Randi follows the directions on her phone and Jack looks out at all the interesting architecture of downtown. "It's sure not Nuevo, is it?"

Randi laughs. "Hardly." She approaches the onramp to the freeway. "Hey, did you apply to any colleges?"

Jack turns toward her. "No. I'm just gonna go to the community college. How about you?"

She glances toward him. "Really? That's what I plan to do, too." She smiles and merges into the slow lane. "I figure I'll take some general ed requirements and dance classes."

"I'm not totally sure what I even *want* to study. So, I'll probably do the same."

"How about a car? Are you saving up for one?"

"No." Jack chuckles. "I don't really *want* one. But I have to say, the public transportation I used this morning leaves much to be desired."

"Weren't you talking about that with Miss Val recently?" The rain has stopped so she turns off the windshield wipers.

"Uh huh. I'd like there to be more options for rides to and from Nuevo. I've been thinking about getting involved in the community to see if the public transit can be upgraded somehow."

"Well, that sounds like a worthy cause to me. You should."

"Yeah, I've gotten more interested in that whole idea lately. Who knows—maybe I'll study *that* in college?"

"And dance?" Randi looks sideways at him.

"Of course," he says, thinking back to the master class they just took. "Especially if I can find classes like we had today."

"Yeah, right? I'm not sure we can get that in school, though. We might have to sign up for master classes through a studio for that."

"Mm hmm, at least for *that* caliber we probably would."

"We could do them together then, if you like?" Randi turns down the heater.

"Absolutely. That was a blast. Do you think they might be offered this summer?"

"I bet there will be." Randi tilts her head from side-to-side, loosening her neck muscles.

"Well then—" Jack grins. "It's a date then?"

Randi smiles back. "Sure."

12

THE TWELVE DANCING PRINCESSES

Julie

Be careful who, or what, you follow.

Julie's hamstrings and calf muscles burn as she executes the last two phrases of the *changements, royales,* and *entrechat quatres* at the end of class. She can barely hold the tight fifth position when she finishes bringing her arms down to first and straightens her knees. Miss Val excuses them and she leans over to brace her hands on her knees, breathing hard. Others do the same and she puts one leg behind at a time to stretch her calf muscles. *Ow.*

"Oh, wait—" Miss Val calls out after stopping the music. "Has everyone turned in their money for the ballet this weekend? I need it today."

Most everyone nods. The only one not there is Jack, who had to leave early.

"All right then. We'll work out rides later. But we're taking you, right, Julie?"

"Yes, please."

Julie joins Sophia and pulls on a skirt over her ballet attire. "I'm so sorry you don't get to go to the ballet. Are you still going to see your grandmother?"

Sophia waves goodbye to Deanne and Brindle as they head out the door to walk to the library. "Lucky ducks," she says under her breath. "Yeah. I have to go right home and try to get *all* my homework done tonight so I can turn it in tomorrow. We're actually leaving Thursday because *mi abuela* is having surgery."

"How long will you be gone?" *Poor Sophia.*

"I'm not totally sure, but I think we're getting back late Sunday night." Sophia stands and picks up her ballet bag and jacket when she sees her mom pull up outside. "See ya."

Julie follows her out the door and the Beginning class starts. "Good luck getting your homework done. Maybe I'll see you at lunch tomorrow."

Miss Val's blue Subaru pulls into the library parking lot and parks next to Mom's car. Brindle waves from the front seat and Julie gets out. The two women talk about meeting back here after the ballet while she gets in next to Willow in the back seat.

She rolls down her window. "Bye, Mom."

"Have a good time. See you later." She waves as Miss Val backs out of the space and they leave the lot.

"So—" Brindle turns around. "Have you read the story about *The Twelve Dancing Princesses*? It's from the Brothers Grimm fairy tale."

"No, but I think I might have seen the Barbie version of it a long time ago."

"It's way better than that." Brindle laughs. "Don't you think, Mom?"

Miss Val smiles. "Well, *I* think so."

Willow joins in, looking at Julie. "I liked the movie version myself."

"Of course, you did, Willow. *You* couldn't sit still long enough to read it." Brindle laughs again. She goes on about the story being about these twelve sisters who are locked in their room every night by their father, the king. But every morning he finds their shoes completely worn out as if they'd been dancing all night. He issues a challenge to anyone who can figure out the riddle of the shoes, offering any one of his daughters in marriage and his kingdom upon his passing.

The group finds their seats in the balcony and Julie gazes over at the gilded boxes, seemingly in place for royalty. Nobody actually sits there, so she wonders what they're really for. She points them out to Brindle, but even she doesn't seem to know. Miss Val is leaning the other way, talking to Willow. Before long, the lights dim and the orchestra below begins to play. The conductor, standing on his podium, looks toward each section and waves his arms smoothly, like a dance. A hush falls over the theater as the music slowly comes to life and the curtains lift magically upward.

The king struts around the stage looking at the pile of worn shoes, pointing and gesturing threateningly. The girls act clueless about the cause of this quandary and move submissively around him. *What a tyrant. I'm glad my dad's not so overbearing.* Brindle points out one of the princesses whispering to another and mocking their father.

Julie nods and whispers, "So many sisters, huh?"

A ripple of laughter travels around them as the antics onstage continue. The king stomps his foot menacingly and yanks up a *pointe* shoe by the ribbons and it flies offstage. *Was that on purpose?* It must *not* have been, because he quickly bends over to retrieve another one and shakes it at his trembling daughters. Between the hysterical pantomiming and the beautiful dancing and stage set, the audience remains captivated as the first act unfolds.

Later, Julie looks on as the twelve sisters dance around the stage bedroom, doing one another's hair, holding up dresses, and playing with ribbons and bows. The atmosphere is lively and festive in anticipation of their upcoming evening out. Julie wonders if Cari had been born sooner, would they have had fun times with each other like this? After much preparation, the dancers disappear through a trap door in the floor and she finds herself wishing she could go with them. *I'd love to go on an adventure like that, even if it is pretend.*

The curtain lowers and the house lights come on. Brindle stands up to stretch. "Do you want to go out to the lobby? It's intermission."

"Sure."

Julie and Brindle squeeze past Miss Val and Willow and follow other patrons down the steps and out the side door to the hallway leading to the main stairs. But when they see the huge glowing chandelier, at eye level, they make their way to the railing to get closer. Julie looks down at the people below, all dressed up in formal attire for this Sunday afternoon at the ballet.

Brindle interrupts her thoughts. "I wonder what each of their stories is." She leans over and peers down into the lobby.

"Um. Maybe they just came to see the ballet?"

"Oh, come on." Brindle grins and nods toward an older man standing in a corner holding a slender glass of champagne. "Do you think he's waiting for his wife to come out of the restroom or—"

Julie gets the drift now. "No, he's just standing there, looking all gentlemanly and everything, trying to get some fine lady to notice him."

They giggle and Brindle tilts her head to another. "How about her?"

"You mean that usher over there?"

"Yeah."

"Well—" Julie begins. "She's got ten kids at home and she's just glad to get away from them for the night and watch at least some of the ballet. How's that?"

"Okay. Is she single or is there a good husband or a deadbeat dad in the picture?"

"Wow, you're really into this, aren't you?"

Paige comes up between them. "Chandelier gazing, are we?"

"Hey," Brindle says. "Where are you guys sitting?"

"Up above you guys," Randi answers.

Paige adds, "In the nosebleed section."

"It's such a funny ballet, isn't it?" Brindle asks.

Randi says, "It is. Hey—isn't that Deanne down there? Who's she with?"

Brindle scans the crowd below. "I think she said she was going with some friends from church. It's too bad Sophia couldn't come. I hope her grandma's doing okay."

"She told me they were going down to TJ because her grandma is getting surgery and they wanted to be there." Julie checks her phone to see if there are any texts. There aren't. "But I think they're coming back tonight."

The lights flash on and off, so they make their way back to their seats. The scene comes to life when the orchestra begins to play. The first two fellows never get to follow the girls through the forest to the ball, succumbing to sleep when the sisters taint their drinks. The third, however, meets an old woman who gives him a magic cloak. With this, he becomes invisible and successfully reports back to the king the truth about the worn-out slippers. This not-so-young man winds up paired with the eldest daughter and will inherit the kingdom when the time comes.

Brindle leans over and whispers, "Why does this nobody get to show up and get everything? The king has *twelve* daughters, after all."

"I know it. Fairy tales will be fairy tales, I guess."

"But the scenery sure is beautiful." Brindle's focus returns to the stage below.

After the *finale*, Paige and Randi come down to meet them.

"So much for women's rights, huh, Brindle?" Paige scoffs.

"Uh huh. Don't any of these ballets showcase feminine strength?"

Miss Val answers. "Only subtly, very subtly. And it's usually only the women who pick up on it."

"That's because we're smarter." Randi laughs and they proceed down toward the lobby as a group.

❧

They've decided to meet at a diner on the way home and Julie is relieved to see Paige and Randi are already there. She's starving and can hardly wait to order. It's cold out, so everyone wants hot cocoa except for Miss Val, who requests tea.

"Could I get the omelet supreme with no onions, please?" Julie notices their teacher and Brindle order salads.

When the waitress leaves, Miss Val asks, "So, how's that baby sister of yours, Julie? I haven't seen her lately."

"Oh, fine. She still doesn't sleep much and she cries a lot."

"Each one is so different. Did you sleep much as a baby? Or cry? Has your mom told you?"

I never thought of that. "Hmm, I don't know." Julie thinks about that nice woman they met in Mexico, who shared food with her family. *And her son had seemed pretty good-natured and helpful.* "I'll have to ask."

Paige cups both hands around her mug. "Do you ever get to babysit? I think it would be so much fun to have a tiny little sister."

"Well, sometimes I take her for short stroller rides while Mom makes dinner. But she's usually too fussy."

"Is she fussy with your mom, too?" Randi asks.

"Yeah, pretty much for all of us. Except when we were on vacation. She actually did pretty well then."

"Maybe because you all were more relaxed. That can make a *big* difference. Babies can sense that," Miss Val says.

Brindle laughs. "I remember how many times I had to read *The Polar Express* to Taz last year. You and Dad were so busy and *way* too stressed out to make the story come to life, like I did. But it was kind of fun—*I guess.*" She smiles teasingly at her mom.

Miss Val opens her mouth to say something, but smiles instead and wraps her fingers around her tea cup. "You're right. You saw a need and you stepped in. Thank you."

"Of course." Brindle grins back at her.

Paige looks over at Julie. "Who knows, what if you helped more with Cari—would your mom be more relaxed then?"

"If only things were that easy," Randi says. "But I'd probably be willing to do it if it would mean less noisy fussing."

"I suppose it's worth a try. I *have* been helping out a little more with her since our trip." Julie tries to picture the results of that. *Maybe it has helped a little.*

"Speaking of pitching in, I have to milk goats when we get home."

"You're so lucky, Brindle!" Randi says.

Willow's been pretty quiet this whole time, but pipes up with, "Well, I have to muck corrals."

"Lucky you, too!" Randi laughs and the others join in. "I help with the housework and we all do our own laundry."

"Chores are important," Miss Val says. "It takes a village, you know."

The food arrives and the conversation wanes while the hungry dancers fortify their appetites. Julie's omelet really hits the spot. Randi and Willow get burgers and Paige is eating a veggie omelet with no cheese.

"Is that any good?" Julie asks.

"It's okay. I don't eat gluten or dairy so this works."

"You seem to be feeling much better this year, aren't you?" Miss Val asks.

"Yeah, as long as I eat what I'm supposed to."

"Well, good for you, Paige. I know it's not always easy."

Julie looks out the large windows and notices it's almost dark. "Should I call my mom yet, Miss Val?"

"How about as soon as we get in the car. Then we'll have a better idea of when we'll get back to the library lot."

On the drive home, Julie thinks of their earlier conversation, about trying to help out more. And then, again, about that wonderful Mexican family that gave so much when they, most likely, had so little. *How could I not have seen how selfish I've been—and so self-centered. Mom shouldn't have to deal with a colicky baby and everything else all by herself. All I ever do at home, practically, is watch anime and hardly ever chip in. Even Willow has more chores than I do.* And with these thoughts, Julie decides she's going to try harder to be a better daughter—and sister.

13

UNDECIDED

Jack

*Dancers are constantly weighing
options. Our awareness extends beyond
the mind and into our bodies.*

By the end of April, the dancers know most of their parts in the ballet, *Coppélia*. Just a few more classes and then they'll start the four full rehearsals where most of the cast will practice together at the studio. Everyone always looks forward to the entire cast dancing together.

"Hey, Jack—how come you didn't go see *The Twelve Dancing Princesses* with us?" Paige asks, carrying the other end of the *barre* with him.

He sets his side down and scoots the stand back with his foot. "I didn't let Miss Val know in time."

"Yeah, he forgot." Randi teases with a grin.

Jack puts up his hands in defense. "You got me. I did forget." He moves out of the way when Todd brings over his *barre*. "Did you go to the ballet?"

"No," Todd says. "I've been super busy at the rental place and I'm trying to get top scores in my AP classes, so I'm studying a lot."

"How are your classes going?" Miss Val asks as she drapes her sweater over the back of the chair.

"Pretty good, I think. I got As on all my midterms."

"Wow, way to go! That's no easy feat," Annie says. "What made you take such hard classes, anyway?"

Typically, Todd has been the class clown, but this year Jack has noticed a change in him. They're still friends, but not nearly as tight as they once were. *I guess we both just got busier.*

"Well—" Todd begins. "I applied to Stanford and Harvard. I haven't heard back yet, but in case I get into one of them, I needed to make sure I had the grades and caliber of classes to follow through."

What? Did I hear right? Todd, who hardly ever studied before, is aspiring to Stanford and Harvard? You've got to be kidding. Jack watches the entire class register their disbelief.

Even Miss Val's mouth hangs open. "When did you decide to apply to those places? I mean, how did we miss this?" She quizzically looks around at her students.

Todd laughs. "I know how it must seem, but I've been working on being a better student for a couple years now. I didn't tell anybody because I wasn't sure if I could do it. I wanted to save myself from possible embarrassment."

Randi says, "*I* didn't even know and we dated most of last year."

"I know, I'm sorry. But I wanted to keep it to myself."

"What do you think you might like to major in?" Jack asks.

Todd clears his throat. "Maybe aerospace engineering or something similar."

"Wow." Jack shakes his head, smirking. "Just when you think you know a guy, huh?"

Paige says, "I'm impressed. Most colleges don't just look at your GPA anymore. They look at the whole picture. And *you* kind of *are* the complete package."

"Yes, you certainly are, Todd," Miss Val says. "Good luck. We're all rooting for you." She looks up at the clock on the wall. "Okay, we better hurry up. Places for the village scene, everyone."

They run through Act One quickly and move on to where Franz is in the toymaker's shop. Unbeknownst to him, Swanilda has dressed in Coppélia's clothes and is acting like she's really the doll. She fools Dr. Coppelius and Franz. The devious doctor gives poor unsuspecting Franz an elixir that puts him into a deep sleep so he can play an evil trick on him. Swanilda, as Coppélia, sees this and repeatedly attempts to save her beloved.

The rest of the class cracks up when Todd pushes Jack down into the chair, tips his head back, and pretends to pour the drink down his victim's throat. Randi, sitting in her chair as the doll, brings both hands up to her face in mock distress. The "doll" shenanigans have already been played out, so she runs over to Jack and tries to shake him awake. Todd forcefully pulls her away and sends her reeling, back to the chair in the corner. Todd maniacally waves his arms around Jack as if casting an evil spell.

Randi gets up again and runs toward them with outstretched arms. She manages to pull Todd away and sends him spinning. He falls down and clammers around hysterically, sending those who are watching into more fits of laughter. Poor Jack is still slumped over, as if sound asleep. Randi pulls him up to standing, but when Todd yanks her back, Jack falls right back into the chair. He snores loudly, not part of the choreography, adding to the hilarity of the scene. This time, when Randi awakens him, he staggers drunkenly around the floor and flails his arms uselessly.

Todd grabs him by the wrist and starts dragging him away from Randi, but she latches onto his other hand and they play tug-of-war with the helpless ragdoll. Jack tones it down a little when whiplash feels imminent. At last, Randi wins and they both fall down into a heap. She rises quickly to fight off Todd, who now is using his cane as a weapon. Ducking under a lethal swing, she pushes the mad doctor down, seizes Jack by the hand, and they flee off stage left. Todd is left standing in the middle of the floor scratching his head, as if dazed and confused.

At the end of the Saturday rehearsal, Jack sticks around while everyone else leaves. He wants to speak with Miss Val without the distraction of others. He's still confused about what he should be doing right now as he nears the end of his high school career. His dad means well, but doesn't really understand, while she's a good listener and often has helpful advice.

"Hey Jack, what's up?" The tall blonde lady always looks more like a dancer than a teacher.

"I still can't make up my mind about what I want to do when I grow up." He grins sheepishly.

Miss Val laughs and turns to face him. "Do you feel like it's something you have to decide right now?"

"Well—I probably should have some idea by now, shouldn't I? I mean, at least some direction."

"Hmm. I think you already do. Aren't you planning to go to the community college in the fall?"

"Yeah, but now that seems so lame—especially after hearing about Todd's plans. Where did that come from, anyway?"

Miss Val shakes her head. "I guess none of us saw that coming. He's always been bright. Maybe he finally discovered that for himself."

Jack shakes his head absentmindedly. "Sometimes I feel about as brainless and unthinking as Copelius' wind-up toys."

She laughs. "Hey—you know how we were talking about the planning meeting where the highway improvement would be on the agenda?"

"Yeah."

She arranges the attendance cards on the desk, puts them into the large manila envelope, and slides it into her briefcase. "I think it's not this week, but the next. I saw it in the paper. Would you still want to go to that?"

"Maybe, but all *they* want to do is make the road wider."

"But *you* might have a better idea than that. Remember?"

"Jack looks out the window at the gleaming cars in the parking lot. "You mean about trying to improve the public transportation here?"

"Yes, that." She stares at him intently.

Is she actually serious about this? "I don't think there's anything *I* can do about it."

"Oh, now I wouldn't be so sure about that. I heard you speak pretty passionately about it the last time we discussed it."

They both turn their heads when raised voices come from right outside.

"What are you talkin' about? Your Chevy ain't faster than my Ford. That's for sure!"

"Prove it!" the other guy argues. "Yer truck's a heap a junk."

The two carry on as they walk farther away, their voices becoming faint.

Jack tips his head toward the parking lot. "But *that's* what I'd be up against. I rest my case."

They both laugh.

"Yes," Miss Val says, turning back toward him. "But not all of Nuevo is like them—luckily."

"No, but a lot of them are," Jack defends. "What would you suggest?"

Miss Val clears her throat. "Well, for one thing, maybe change the situation by taking action."

"Meaning?"

"Why not sign up to talk at the meeting?"

"Me?"

"Sure. Why not?"

"Because I'd probably sound like an idiot."

"Not if you do your homework." Miss Val takes the long black sweater from the back of the chair and puts it on. "Who knows, maybe Nuevo could become more of a hub. Lots of visitors come through here, on the way to the desert or to go to the snow."

Jack mulls this over a moment. "M-a-y-b-e."

"And *maybe* that's your new direction. Who knows? It might become your vocation, or a major in college or—" She raises her dark eyebrows.

"Hmm. You've definitely given me more things to think about. *Again*. Thanks, Miss Val."

As Jack leaves, he decides to ride his bike the long way home so he can have more time to think. Not that it's that busy at home or anything. But Dad usually only works a half day on Saturdays and right now he just wants to be by himself for a while.

That evening, they dig into their takeout pizza and Dad asks, "So, how was your day?"

"Good." Jack finishes chewing. "Hey, Dad? Have you ever been to one of those planning meetings?"

"Yeah, why?"

"I was just wondering what they're like."

"Long. I had to go quite a while ago to get my business approved."

"Oh." Jack gets up to pour a glass of milk. "I heard they'll be talking about widening the road at the next one. I might want to go check it out."

Dad looks at him when he sits back down. "Does this have anything to do with your sudden interest in taking the bus and trolley to San Diego?"

"Yeah, sort of."

"Interesting." Dad tips back his chair, smiling, as if having a pleasant memory, or slowly getting an idea. He doesn't say anything for quite a while, but that's fine, since the two of them have become comfortable in each other's silence. Neither feels the need to fill the space with useless chatter. And Jack always feels accepted and appreciated by his quiet demeaner. Finally, Dad stands to clear the table. "You know what, son? You never cease to surprise me. From that look in your eye, I sense you might be on to something." He picks up the empty pizza box and grins. "Whatever it is, I'll leave you to it."

"Thanks, Dad. I think I'll go do some research in my room."

"Okay then. I'll go ahead and lock up. Good night."

Dad's reassuring presence, and Miss Val's words, have, as usual, given him a lot to think about. *This planning meeting might be interesting.* He opens his laptop and looks up "Public Transportation in San Diego." One thing leads to another and before long he has ten tabs open. Jack's surprised at how much information there is about San Diego transportation.

It turns out there used to be several more bus runs offered during the day between Nuevo and various parts of San Diego. Due to lack of ridership, most of them were discontinued. *That's too bad. Why aren't more commuters using the transit system?* He surmises if they continue to widen the roads, then everyone will just keep driving. While reading on, he becomes more and more enamored with the idea that maybe he actually might be able to make a difference and possibly even instigate policy change.

But who am I kidding? Did all this start with me breaking down all the time in that old jalopy I used to drive? Then he thinks of his econ class and how disgruntled he's become since learning that the success of a society is dependent on continuous economic growth. *That's not even possible in the long run, is it?* He ponders these questions as he reads further. *Of course, people aren't going to make use of public transportation if it doesn't take them where they want to go or it takes too long to get there.* He runs his fingers through his hair and asks himself aloud, "What's that saying? Oh yeah, 'If you build it, they will come.'"

Jack leans back and smiles, thinking of his and Dad's favorite movie of all time, *Field of Dreams*. It's where that saying came from, at least that's where he heard it. The guy in the film listened to that voice in his head and created a baseball field out in the middle of nowhere. *If you build it, they will come. Nuevo isn't nowhere.* And it's at this moment that Jack decides to take action to try to change the situation, as Miss Val says. *I'm going to need to gather as much information as I can about this and go to that meeting! Maybe I can make a difference after all.*

14

THE PAIN OF POINTE

Julie

Anything really worth doing
requires diligence and hard work.

By the eighth *relevé*, Julie's toes are on fire. Clutching the *barre*, she tries to pull her feet upward, but Miss Val keeps talking about pushing down into the floor to go up. It's all so confusing. *Thirteen, fourteen, two more to go—but I can't.* She bends over the *barre*, picking up one foot at a time and shaking it out. "Oohh." The others are managing fine, it seems, but they have all been at it longer than she has. This is only Julie's fifth or sixth time with her new *pointe* shoes.

Miss Val cuts the music at the end of the exercise and walks over. "Don't worry, Julie, you'll get it. It's a lot harder than it looks, isn't it?"

"Uh huh. Why does it have to hurt so much?" She tries to rub her toes, but it has no effect, other than to get her fingers sticky from the rosin on the hard box of her shoe.

Miss Val reminds her of the importance of straightening her knees completely after the *plié* before rising onto *pointe*. "We wouldn't want to start any bad habits now. They're much more difficult to break later." She smiles and demonstrates the next exercise. Julie is to continue facing the *barre* and holding on with both hands while the others step out onto the floor for *échappés*.

The music begins and Julie *pliés* in fifth to prepare. She shoots out her feet determinedly toward second position *en relevé*, but only the right foot goes up all the way. Her left flounders *en demi-pointe*. She grips the *barre* for a stronger hold. *Why can't I do this?* On the next try it is exactly opposite. *My feet just don't slide out evenly.* She watches Randi and Deanne do theirs effortlessly. Brindle's, Annie's, and Sophia's aren't bad, either. Her seventh one isn't awful, but the last is nonexistent. She just can't make it up again.

Miss Val finally calls an end to the *barre*. Julie was ready two exercises ago and she knows she couldn't have done one more thing *en pointe*. She hobbles over toward her ballet bag, grateful that Jack offers to carry the *barre*. Her feet are killing her and she's not sure she'll ever be able to walk normally again.

Sophia plops down next to her. "You're getting better."

Julie pulls off the right shoe and gently rubs her sensitive toes. "It sure doesn't feel like it. Why didn't you tell me it hurts this much?"

Sophia drinks before answering. "Didn't I?"

"Not that I remember." She grimaces and grins at the same time, which makes Brindle laugh.

"It does get easier."

"But it's never totally easy," Annie adds. "It's just not what you thought it would be like. In fact, I think we all went through that."

Paige scoots closer. "Hey—maybe it's like the story, *To Kill A Mockingbird*."

"Huh?" Deanne makes a face. "That's kind of random."

Julie turns toward a *staccato* pattering and sees Randi doing quick little *bourrées* across the floor with Jack following behind.

"No, really. Do you remember how those kids chose to believe certain things about Boo Radley, like he was so cruel and spooky? And then in the end, after meeting him, they found out he wasn't that way at all."

Brindle raises her dark eyebrows as if a lightbulb comes on in her mind. "Mm hmm, that's true."

"Yup, we can't always know something before we've experienced it, can we?"

Deanne laughs. "You're such a bookworm, Paige."

"I'm just sayin'."

They all giggle, and Julie appreciates how candid they all can be with each other. One more cool thing about this place, she decides, and gratefully puts on her soft ballet slippers for the rehearsal to begin.

The group assembles to practice the dance in which Dr. Coppelius loses his key. Randi asks, "Are the squirrels going to be in this ballet, Miss Val?"

She looks up from her choreography notebook. "Of course, they are. What would a Dance Centre story ballet be without the squirrels?"

Todd snorts. "Is there actually a part for them in *Coppélia?*"

"No, but in our version there is." She smiles mischievously. "You know, how in those old fairy tales, there are often rats that rummage through the city streets at night?"

"Y-e-a-h," Paige says, grinning with anticipation.

"I know," Jack interrupts. "We'll have squirrels instead of rats, right?"

"Yes," she says, beaming. "You all are finally getting the hang of this, aren't you?"

And with laughter and razzing, the dance begins. As Franz, Jack teases and pushes Todd. He pretends his sidekicks are with him, but they haven't practiced together yet. He points for one to kick, motions for another to go around, and then spins the mad toymaker in circles until he's so dizzy, he falls down. Todd pretends to drop the giant key, since they don't have the actual one yet, and staggers off.

Swanilda and her friends enter from stage left and she immediately gets after her beloved for flirting with Coppélia and harassing the old man. She angrily pushes him and forces him to leave, hopeless and helpless. Of course, now that Franz is gone, she absolutely must go meet this strange girl who always seems to be sitting in the window, trying to entice him away. The group of girls dance together, as if in the street below the window.

Randi *finds* the, as yet, nonexistent key and jumps up and down excitedly. She proceeds to pretend to unlock the door and sneak into the room with her friends in tow. It's a fun segment and Julie wishes they were actually doing something like this for real. *They always have all the fun in these fairy tales. Why not in real life?* The dance that follows is the one with all the toys, which, of course, is so silly that it's a blast. They all have a good time with it.

Far too quickly, class is over and it's time for the Beginners. Julie goes out with Sophia and the others, and they sit down out front on the sidewalk. Jack takes off on his bike and Todd gets a ride with Annie to the rental equipment shop where he works. Randi starts talking about the slumber party she's hosting for all of them. She does this every year so the Advanced cast can bond and have fun together a few weeks before the performances. But not the guys— it's just for the girls.

"I think my dad's going to order pizza."

Paige says, "I'll bring something I can eat."

"I'll bring a vegan main dish," Brindle offers.

Cars pull out of the parking lot as Deanne's mother turns in. "Bye, guys. See you Saturday. Hey Brindle— are we having a longer rehearsal that day?"

Brindle shakes her head. "Not that I know of."

As Deanne leaves, Randi says, "You guys can bring whatever you'd like, too. Also, what ballet movie should we watch, *Coppélia*?"

"Of course," Sophia answers. "What other?"

"It sounds like so much fun," Julie says. "I'm sorry I missed it last year. Did you guys watch *The Nutcracker*?"

"Of course." Randi smiles. "I can't believe it will be my last time hosting this."

"And my last time going. You ready?" Paige drapes her arm over Randi's shoulder.

"Yup." Randi gathers her things and the two of them walk to her car.

Brindle asks Julie how her feet are feeling.

"Huh?" She hasn't thought about them since taking her *pointe* shoes off. "Oh, I hadn't noticed. Fine, I guess."

"Funny how that is, isn't it? Speedy recovery from utterly intense pain."

Julie's phone chimes and she reads her mom's text about running late. While her phone's in hand, she touches a shiny pink icon. "Do you guys know this game?" She turns her cell around and points to the screen. "It's so great. It's about—"

Brindle stands up and waves when Mr. Val, as they all refer to him, stops in front of the building. Willow bolts out of the car and into the studio, as usual. She'll have a little while to wait before the Intermediate class starts. Brindle says, "Sorry, Julie. Sophia can tell you about how I feel about computer games. See ya."

"What was that about anyway?"

Sophia sighs. "Well—Brindle thinks they're a waste of time. And they're not even *real*, whatever *that* means."

"Really? But this one's so awesome. There's these kids who dance, even juggle, to save the whales."

"And it's a game? Let me see," Sophia says, taking the phone from her.

"The more dance moves your character achieves, the closer they get to attaining their goal."

"That's cool."

"They get money for each successful move. And if the move is more complicated, then it's worth more." Julie points at the screen in Sophia's hand.

Sophia stares at it. "Hey, I watched one of the episodes from that anime series you sent me the link to. It's pretty funny."

Julie thinks for a moment, trying to remember which one. "Oh yeah. It is, isn't it?"

The Hernandez's van pulls up and Sophia hands back the phone. She gets up to leave, but turns back. "I'll see you Saturday, okay?"

"All right." Julie tosses the phone in her bag and leans back into the wall. As Sophia's family drives away, Julie listens to the music coming from inside the studio, behind her. The Beginners are practicing their villager dance.

Coppélia *isn't real*. Julie thinks about Brindle's attitude. *Why does she seem so against gaming?* Julie closes her eyes and then remembers why she's here. She loves to dance. These kids are her friends. And the story ballets are something they actually *do* together. They cocreate a cohesive work of art.

Mom drives up and Julie gets into the car. "How about if *I* make dinner tonight?"

"Hah, really?"

"Yes, really. How about spaghetti and garlic bread?"

"That sounds marvelous," Mom says, turning to smile at her. "I can't wait."

15

The Meeting

Jack

*Take a chance! Why not go
for that extra turn?*

Jack really hadn't given much thought to civic involvement before, at least prior to talking with Miss Val about road and transportation issues. It may have begun with that blasted old Honda that kept breaking down and leaving him stranded. Or it could have had something to do with his econ class, and learning the commonly held belief that if a business or economy doesn't grow, it's destined to fail. *What about when the collapse of 2008 happened and the business empires that were "too big to fail" crashed and brought shareholders and innocent bystanders down with them?*

Why is ridership on public transportation down in the U.S.? At least that's what his research shows. He supposes when automotive companies are committed to the practice of encouraging ever-more consumer debt, making the use of personal vehicles affordable for so many, there's not much incentive to be inconvenienced by *sharing* rides or getting by with less. And, of course, there's the massive environmental destruction that goes hand-in-hand with that mindset. He wonders if there's any hope at all for the future, but decides he'll at least go to this town planning meeting and see what happens. But first, he must prepare.

Jack spends most the weekend poring over statistics concerning mass transit use in San Diego County. He studies maps with various routes distinguished by different colors and finds connection sites for transfers. After a while, it reminds him of what a floor plan for a dance might look like. If observed from above the stage, the dancer travels back and forth and around in circles, which creates something similar to a finger painting he would have done back in kindergarten. He chuckles at the thought and realizes how off course he's getting.

What am I doing anyway? I don't really know anything about this. All I want is for people to see there could be a very good alternative to widening the highway, which would add even more car exhaust and toxic fumes to our country town's mountain air. Doesn't anyone care about that?

He continues his search for pertinent information to help his cause and eventually goes off on another tangent. *How is "big" necessarily better? It sure doesn't guarantee better service. Sometimes the smaller shops are more personal and give superior service. That's why I would want to go back and support* them. *Dad does that. And* his *shop is one of those "small businesses." He's got quite a loyal following.* Then Jack thinks of the Dance Centre and how, by keeping it fairly small, Miss Val is able to personally connect with each and every student.

As he clicks through screens on his laptop, a page on sports injuries comes up. As he distractedly reads about conditions like tendinitis, torn rotator cuffs, and golfer's elbow, he starts talking to himself. "It's even true about athletics. One can actually *overdo* an exercise trying to get better, or bigger, and hurt themselves. Jeez—people are so stupid." *Enough of this. Time for food.*

❧

Sooner than Jack feels prepared for, the evening of the town planning meeting arrives and he signs up to speak on the road issue. Dad's here with him and he's surprised when Miss Val slides into the seat next to them.

"I didn't know you were coming."

"It's an important topic. And you're presenting, so of course I'm here."

"Hello, Val. It's good to see you." Dad smiles and looks around the crowded room.

The president of the planning board calls the meeting to order and announces the items on the agenda. Unfortunately, the road topic is at the end. The folks in the audience, made up mostly of concerned citizens who are directly involved with one or more of tonight's discussions, await their turn in the uncomfortable folding metal chairs. Over an hour later, the road item is called.

The president informs the group that quite a few people have signed up to speak, so each person will have up to three minutes. "When the timer goes off, please just finish your sentence and go back to your seat. First up, we have Carl Baker, the owner of Gas & Go."

A man in a ballcap and overalls goes up to the microphone and clears his throat. "Howdy, everybody. I'm sure we all want what's best for the town and that means safer roads. Am I right?" He goes on promoting the widening of the highway to cut the number of fatalities.

Jack listens to his argument, along with others just like it, feeling more and more nervous as his turn approaches. "No one wants to hear what I have to say," he whispers to Miss Val.

"You don't know that for sure until you try. What you have to say is worth them hearing." She smiles warmly and pats his shoulder. "You've got this, Jack."

And then his name is called and he stands up on wobbly legs. Walking to the podium, he sincerely wishes he'd never signed up for this. He introduces himself and hears his voice shake. "Well, I'm not here to talk about widening the road or anything like that. In fact, I'm against it. And I'm not the only one, but probably the only one you'll hear from." Jack nods to his dad and Miss Val, who grin back at him. He continues to talk about never expanding the road, but instead, having just one lane in each direction.

A few scoff and comment about how ridiculous it would be. "How's *that* supposed to work?" And others mumble what a crazy, unacceptable idea he has. "It won't allow for growth in our community!"

"Just hold on and hear me out." Jack puts up his hand in defense. "If we believe growth is inevitable, that's another reason *not* to do it. Instead, I think we should put a light rail system down the middle of the existing road."

Now there are more disapproving reactions and the president's gavel hits the table. "That's enough. Let the young man have his say." He glares at the most vocal guy. "We heard you out, Carl. It's this fellow's turn now." He nods to Jack. "Go on."

"It doesn't seem like it's a good idea, to me, to just continue to make roads bigger and bigger. It's not sustainable. And it will carve up more and more of our beautiful countryside. Let's just bite the bullet and put in public transportation now, and eventually, those who don't want to sit in traffic will start using it."

"It's *way* too expensive! Have you thought about that?"

Jack holds up a finger. "Yes—it's very expensive. But I believe we should be forward-thinking about this and not just keep putting Band-Aids on an ever-increasing problem. Let's invest in our future now and stop throwing money away." He decides to leave it at that. "Thank you for your time."

Heads shake disapprovingly while Miss Val and Dad tell him what a good job he did. The next speaker goes up and ridicules Jack's notions, though semi-politely.

The meeting finally adjourns and Jack can't wait to get out of there. As he exits the end of the row of chairs, a man stops him.

"You got a minute?"

"I guess so."

He starts asking him if he's ever traveled to Europe or Japan and ridden their public transportation.

"No, I haven't. But it sounds great. I've never been out of the country, except down to Mexico a few times."

"It is great," the stranger says. "You're on to a good thing. But unfortunately, I don't think these folks are ready for this yet."

"They may never be."

The man, who's introduced himself—but Jack has already forgotten his name—asks if he knows what a WWOOFer is.

Jack crinkles his nose in confusion. "Isn't it part of a speaker or something?"

The guy laughs. "Well, I suppose it is. But I was referring to volunteers who help out on organic farms in trade for food and lodging. It's a worldwide organization where you can experience living in other countries inexpensively and get in with the culture." He grins. "You know—in case you do want to travel somewhere."

"Huh. I've never heard of it before. Sounds interesting, though."

"You might want to check it out. Maybe experience what some other countries have, like mass transit. We could learn a lot from them—and it might buy you some credibility, at least more than you have right now, in their eyes anyway, as a high school student. Anyway, I gotta run. Good luck with everything." The stranger takes his leave and follows the crowd out of the room.

Jack turns to Miss Val. "Have you heard of that organization?"

"What, WWOOF? I have. It stands for Worldwide Opportunities on Organic Farms. From what I hear, it's a great program."

Jack starts mulling this over in his mind.

Dad gives him a nudge. "Maybe that's what you ought to do this summer, eh?"

Miss Val agrees. "You've been wondering about what direction you want to go after high school. Maybe this is it, at least for the summer. Or, who knows—a year even. As long as you keep dancing."

He laughs. "Kind of like a gap year?"

She smiles. "Perhaps."

The wheels start turning in Jack's head. "Well, I'm probably not getting anywhere arguing for public transportation in this town. At least not for a while. They probably do think I'm just some dumb kid who doesn't know anything. Should I not have tried?"

"You did good, son. Don't beat yourself up."

"Your dad's right. Never *not* try something just because you're afraid to fail. If nothing else, you planted a seed. They may not be ready to change their minds right now, but after tonight they might be more likely to cogitate on it."

"Cogitate?" Dad chuckles. "Good one."

For some reason, Jack flashes on the book, *The Giver*, and turns to Miss Val. "I guess I'd have to work a lot harder to convince them to see the light, huh? Like what Jonas had to go through to save them all."

Miss Val laughs. "Well, I hope you don't have to go to *those* extremes to do it."

The three of them leave the building together and Jack watches his ballet teacher walk to her truck. *How did she get to be so smart?*

Even though it's late when they get home, Jack's curiosity about WWOOFers leads him to his laptop. *At least farming is good physical work and I'd get to be outside. And m-a-y-b-e there might be a dance studio nearby. France, Germany, China, Japan, Italy?*

Jack starts wondering about the synchronicity of the evening. Not exactly his presentation itself, but what happened afterward. Was it *because* of his words to the audience in the room? *If not for that, would that man have stopped to talk with me? It's almost eerie. Hey Mom, are you seeing this?* Because of what happened less than an hour ago, Jack finds himself *potentially* on a new path. *Where will it lead?*

16

PARTY ON

Julie

So many ballets, so many
stories, so many decisions…

Math has never been Julie's strong suit. Polygons, quadrilaterals, cylinders… even decagons swirl through her field of vision until she slams shut the geometry book she's been unproductively studying for the past hour. "Ugh! I'll never get this." She fights off tears because of her inability to comprehend the complicated equations and theorems. There's a big test tomorrow and she can't afford another C. And now the tears are winning.

She wishes she could ask someone for help. Mom's at the store, but she probably doesn't remember much about tenth grade geometry. Then she thinks of Sophia, but she's only a freshman. Not that she'd be any help, but it would be nice not to have to be alone right now. She gets up to go to the kitchen for a drink of water and her phone jingles. It's just junk, but the sound reminds her of the newest song on her playlist. *That's what I need right now.* "It's time to rock out, Julie," she tells herself.

As the melody fills the space, she turns up the volume—way up—and pushes her chair under the desk, clearing the dance floor. The bass pulses and the lamp on her dresser rattles. *Boom-boom-boom-boom.* Her head bobs up and down while her fists punch the air. She closes her eyes tightly and loses herself in the song. Opening her eyes, Julie's entire body joins in the dance: swaying, wiggling, and spinning into oblivion. Her right arm follows the left and creates snake-like movements, while her legs move like Elvis Presley's when he sang *Hound Dog.*

She dances around the room with increasingly wild moves, chasing away things like geometry and a noisy little sister. It feels so good that the waterworks return, but this time they are tears of joyful abandon. She shouts out the lyrics, "Can't wait to run down the beach—hand-in-hand—fall in the sand—" When the song ends, she flops down on the bed, breathing hard.

When the next one starts, she rolls off and immediately spins around on one foot, in *plié,* so she can maintain her balance on the carpet. When the words suggest "getting down," she tucks her chin and summersaults over. A little dizzy, she shakes her head and does it again and again and again—right out her doorway and down the hall. "Wee!" she cries.

Where the rug ends and the tile begins, she decides to summersault backward. This is a little slower going to avoid bumping into walls. She groans when the song ends, but with the first notes of another of her favorites, she goes for another lap down the "speedway." "Whew, am I dizzy." Julie turns back toward her room and dance crawls, bouncing her spine up and down with the beat.

She lies on her back, next to the bed, and moves to the rhythm with just her arms and legs. This allows her to catch her breath. "Hm hmm hmmm," she hums along.

"It looks like you're having fun." Mom's voice appears from nowhere.

Julie looks over. "Oh, I didn't hear you come in."

"Of course, you didn't. It's so loud in here."

Julie turns down the volume. "Where's Cari?"

"In the kitchen. I didn't want her eardrums to burst." Mom lingers. "I thought you had to study for a test."

"I did, but it wasn't going very well so I decided to dance instead."

"Interesting." Mom smiles and takes her leave.

Julie rubs her face and then rolls onto her stomach. Breathing hard, she realizes how much better she feels now. Dancing it out works pretty well.

Randi opens the door and exuberantly welcomes Julie and Sophia in. "You guys are the first ones here to our annual ballet slumber party."

"I brought *sopapillas.*" Sophia holds up a white bag. "Some are sweet and a few have meat in them."

"Mmm," Randi says. "Sounds good."

Julie closes the door behind her. "Well, I didn't bring anything nearly as exotic as her. Just chips and salsa."

"Those are good, too." Randi ushers them into the bright yellow kitchen, where they put their snacks on the large island. The doorbell rings and their host excuses herself.

"I wonder who's here now?"

"Maybe Brindle? Let's lay out our stuff," Sophia suggests.

An old beagle pads into the kitchen and Julie kneels down to pet him. "Oh, you're so cute." He gratefully accepts the attention and licks her hand.

Brindle and Deanne appear in the kitchen, followed by Paige.

Paige bends over and the dog goes to greet her. "Hi, Tortoise. How you doin', old man?" He leans against her leg and pants noisily.

"What did you guys bring?" Sophia asks.

Deanne says she brought chocolate chip cookies and then teases, "But who knows about Brindle and Paige? Probably something *healthy.*"

The girls laugh and Brindle peels back the foil on the baking dish. "Yup. Lentil and Brussels sprout casserole."

"With your homemade cashew cheese?" Paige asks. When Brindle nods, she responds, "Yes! I love that stuff. I had to study physics today so I didn't have much time; I just have a store-bought veggie tray with hummus."

"It's all good," Randi says. "We ordered three kinds of pizza and they should be here any minute."

The group lays out the assorted dishes and Annie waltzes in. "The pizza guy's here—and he's kinda cute."

"Let's go see!" Randi giggles and hurries out to meet him with the pack of girls following.

Deanne rushes to the window and opens the curtain to look outside.

"Well—is he?" Sophia asks.

"*I* think he is."

"Move over then, I wanna see." Sophia peers over Deanne's shoulder.

The girls laugh and Brindle and Julie move toward the window. "Hey, could you move over?" Julie asks, grinning.

Annie comes into the living room after leaving her contribution in the kitchen. "He is, isn't he?"

"Darn right." Deanne opens the door so Randi can carry in the pizzas.

As soon as they close the door, they all crack up and crowd at the window to watch the cute guy drive away.

"Did you see his gorgeous blue eyes?" Deanne squeals.

"Of course," Annie says. "And those cute dimples."

They all lose it again and Randi's mom peeks in from the kitchen.

"What's going on out here? You girls seem to be having *way* too much fun."

"It's just the pizza guy, Mom. He's super good looking." They all laugh again and march into the kitchen.

"Aah, well that explains it then." She smiles and tells them about the two ice cream cakes she just got. "And how are all you girls this evening?"

"Excited," Paige answers for everyone. "And hungry."

Ms. Boles surveys the loaded island. "Evidently."

Randi opens the pizza boxes and points out the plates, napkins, and drinks. In short order, they each dish up their own choices and move to the living room. Julie scans the tidy area—no litter of rattles and stuffed animals, no baby swing, just everything in its place. Except now, she notices her dance family happily filling the space with good cheer and camaraderie.

"What's that you're drinking, Brindle?" Annie asks, deliberately taking a tiny bite of a carrot stick.

"Kombucha with a hint of cinnamon. It's really tasty. Would you like to try it?"

"What is it?" Randi looks across at the bottle of murky liquid.

"Do you really want to know?"

Annie and the others focus on Brindle's academic explanation.

"It's a fermented kind of tea made with sugar, bacteria, and yeast. Some people call it mushroom tea because the mother SCOBY sort of looks like one. It has a lot of health benefits like boosting your immune system. I added cinnamon to this one."

"You made that? Is it alcoholic?" Deanne crinkles her nose.

Brindle holds it up to the light for her little show-and-tell episode. "Yes, I made it. I keep the SCOBY in our refrigerator. And it *is* fermented, but almost no alcohol is produced in the process." She looks around at everyone. "Would you guys like to try it? I brought an extra one."

They all tentatively nod and "mm hmm." Randi goes to the kitchen to retrieve some cups and Brindle pulls another bottle from her bag.

"This one's infused with pomegranate." The cups are set on the coffee table and Brindle pours the red liquid into each. When they all have drinks in hand, Brindle raises her own bottle. "Cheers."

They each take a small sip as if participating in an official tasting of some rare liqueur.

"Well, what do you think?"

"It's interesting," Paige says, licking her lips for clarity.

"It's okay," Annie offers.

"I don't like the bubbles," Deanne says.

Sophia laughs. "Well, it's not my cup of tea, either, but to each his own, right?"

Julie nods and the friends politely finish their shot-sized tastings as Brindle tells them how she feeds sugar to the mother every few days to keep her alive and producing.

Randi starts talking about which production of *Coppélia* she's selected for them to watch tonight. "I've heard not all versions are the same."

"Isn't that how it usually is?" Julie asks.

"I guess, kind of. You guys ready?"

Paige and Brindle go back into the kitchen for seconds, while Randi fiddles with the TV remote.

Randi's mom walks into the room and over to the large window. "Would you like me to close these?"

"Oh, yeah. Thanks." Randi pushes play while Ms. Boles closes the drapes and heads back into the kitchen.

After a few movie previews, the ballet finally starts. Symphonic music floods the room from the surround sound.

"That sounds awesome," Sophia says. "I wish we had that at my house."

Julie nods in agreement and the curtain on the screen rises, revealing what Julie had assumed would be the village scene. But instead, an old man gives a smoldering pipe to the guy in a chair. Coppélia sits motionless in the window. Later, Swanilda and her friends dance in the street and notice the girl in the window.

Randi comments about how festive and lively the music is.

"I'm not completely sure if it's a fast waltz or—maybe it's in 6/8 time?"

Deanne turns to Brindle. "Huh, I don't know, either."

The group watches in awe as the village scene comes alive and Franz and Swanilda celebrate.

"They're so good," Julie says, setting her cup on the coffee table and leaning back onto the sofa cushions.

Sophia talks with her mouth full of pepperoni pizza. "They're amazing."

"Well, they are a professional company, after all." Annie is now munching on a celery stick. "And that Franz guy is pretty cute, isn't he?"

"Mm hmm," Randi hums. "Is that all you're going to eat—rabbit food?"

"I don't know. We'll see. I have an audition for a commercial next week so I'm trying to be extra good."

"You already look great," Paige says. "Can't you live a little sometimes?"

"Ha! Coming from a person who doesn't eat dairy *or* gluten," Deanne scoffs.

"One shouldn't take diet for granted. It does matter what we put into our bodies," Brindle asserts.

"*And* what we do *to* our bodies." Paige smiles confidently.

"Okay, enough already!" Annie suggests they get back to watching the ballet.

Julie laughs at Dr. Coppelius' funny antics. "They sure found a perfect fit for him, didn't they?"

"He's hysterical." Sophia practically spills her popcorn laughing when Swanilda is passed back and forth between the two men and dances dizzily from it.

"So much for feminine composure." Deanne lowers herself to the floor and stretches out onto her stomach.

The end is totally different in this rendition. Franz rescues Swanilda and there's puffs of magic smoke. The two young lovers dance their *pas de deux* and the rest of the cast fades into the background.

"That's not like ours at all," Deanne exclaims.

"No, it certainly isn't," Paige says. "I like our story line way better."

Everyone agrees wholeheartedly and heads to the kitchen for dessert.

"Chocolate peanut butter ice cream cake!" Randi sings in a chipper soprano voice.

"My favorite!" Julie cries and they stand around the large island and devour the entire thing in a matter of minutes. "So good."

Brindle and Paige were clued in ahead of time and Ms. Boles had picked up a small vegan cake as well.

"Ours is really good, too," Paige says, and Brindle echoes the sentiment.

Randi leads the crew in cleaning up and announces, "Dance party as soon as the kitchen detail is done!" This is motivation enough for everyone to pick up the pace.

Deanne helps Randi select the playlist, and the coffee table and extra chairs are pushed to the side. The first song is one they all know and the group of teenagers bounce around like a bunch of kangaroos—at least that's what Julie feels like. The next piece encourages more full body movement so she and Sophia mirror each other's waving arms and body contortions. Giggling ensues when they accidently bump into each other and almost fall down.

Julie loses herself in the moment and pictures dancing the night away with a young, handsome prince. As she immerses her mind, body, and spirit into the music, time slows down and almost ceases to exist. *I have fun when I dance by myself at home, but it's nothing like this. I wish this could go on forever.*

17

AGAIN?

Jack

*Have you had your apple, or
other healthy food, today?*

Jack's bicycle bumps over the ruts in the dirt road. He hasn't attempted this before, but on this beautiful May morning he'd had no other choice for transportation. Not wanting to break his promise to Miss Val about helping out at the cabin today, he's riding his bike all the way from town to her place out in the sticks—about eight miles. It's not far if you're a true cyclist, but a little more challenging on an older mountain bike. But it feels good.

He gets off to open and close the gate, walks the Schwinn over to a rock in the front yard, and props it against it. His backpack, which had seemed pretty light when he'd left, now feels as if it's loaded with stones. Lugging it up the front steps, he pauses for an alligator lizard to scurry away. The doors are never locked out here, so Jack lets himself in, sets his load down in the corner, and thinks about what to start on.

Sand the putty spots in the window trims? Wait, when did those *get here?* He stares at the stack of beautifully stained interior doors leaning against the soon-to-be master bedroom wall. He runs his hand along the surface of the one in front and admires the unique grain in the wood.

"Do you like those?"

Jack turns around to see his ballet teacher in the front doorway, holding two steaming mugs.

"Yeah, they're really nice."

"I picked out a stain that I thought would bring out the grain. I think it did, don't you?"

"Absolutely." Jack continues to stroke the surface. "When did you do these?"

"On Friday. It took me all day to get both coats on, so I didn't get anything else done," she says, walking over to hand him one of the mugs. "Here, it looks like you could use some sustenance after your long trek from town."

"Thanks. What is it?" He takes the blue mug from her.

"Green tea. Maybe it will give you a boost so you can get a lot done this morning." She smiles and sits down on an upside-down bucket and motions for him to do the same. "Take a minute and drink your tea."

"Okay." He obliges and gratefully takes part in the impromptu morning tea party with his ballet teacher.

"So, how's it going for you these days?" Miss Val takes a sip and looks over the rim of her mug at him.

"Oh, you'll never guess." He pauses. "This guy called me last night. He wants me to speak at the planning meeting downtown."

"Downtown San Diego? How did he know about you? Was he at the meeting the other night?"

"Mm hmm. Can you believe it? I told him I thought it's a lost cause, so why?"

"And?" Miss Val raises her dark eyebrows.

"He said what I have to say is important."

"It is."

"I told him I didn't have any more information than what I already said. But he told me I could just say the same things I did before, because sometimes it's important to simply say it again. He thinks it's a good idea, too."

There's rustling in a pile of insulation and a squirrel pops out and runs out the open door. They both laugh and shake their heads.

"But I was *so* nervous. I'm not sure I want to go through that again—and now at a bigger meeting, in the city?" Jack's heart skips a beat just thinking about it.

"But I thought you did a pretty good job. And you wouldn't even have to come up with any new material. I know it's getting to be a busy time with our rehearsals and performances coming up so soon and then finals after that. *And* your work here." She waves her arm around the room.

"Yeah—I don't know."

"Well, give it some thought, Jack. I think you ought to do it. If nothing else, it's good experience—for whatever you decide to pursue later on." She stands up and reaches for his empty mug.

The Australian Shepherd, Nutkins, bounds in, followed by Brindle. "Oh, hi Jack. I didn't know you were here."

"Yup. I rode my bike."

"Hey, Mom? Is it okay if Deanne comes over to play music with me this afternoon?"

"Wow, you guys haven't done that in a long time. Sure."

"Play music?" Jack asks.

"Mm hmm. Deanne has a clarinet and I play piano—well, small keyboard now because that's all we have room for in the trailer. We used to do it pretty often, but with me homeschooling and her getting more into the whole school scene—we haven't had much time."

"Huh. Sounds fun." Jack picks up a paintbrush and starts applying clearcoat to the living room window trim.

Miss Val heads outside with Brindle and Nutkins.

Jack can hardly believe it's the last of the four full rehearsals at the studio and the dress rehearsal and upcoming concert are *this* week. "Wasn't it just Christmas, like yesterday?"

Randi agrees. "And it's amazing that our high school careers are almost behind us, huh? I don't think I'm ready."

"But you're ready for *this*, right?" Paige asks, coming up behind them.

"What?" Randi asks.

"Your roles as the lovely Swanilda and the handsome prince, Franz."

The stage couple laughs and Miss Val reminds them how to behave around the younger kids when they get here. "In the meantime, do your best to cement your dances into muscle memory, okay?"

They continue to stretch and Todd scooches over toward Jack and Randi.

"I got in." His gigantic smile practically takes over his whole face.

"Where?" Randi asks.

"To Stanford!" He continues grinning, nods excitedly, and starts to laugh.

Randi leans over and hugs him. "Congratulations. I'm so proud of you."

"Yeah—way to go, dude." Jack slaps him on the back.

Miss Val overhears and tells him what a great achievement it is and proceeds to lead the class in song: "For he's a jolly good fellow."

The entire group joins in to celebrate their typically silly friend's acceptance into such a prestigious university. Todd beams unabashedly, soaking up the attention and goodwill of his comrades.

When the last lingering note ends, he thanks them for their support. "You know," he begins his impromptu speech. "I could *not* have done it without all of you—each and every one. You're like my family."

His voice cracks, but he acts quite serious. Everyone busts up because that's just how he does things. He knows how to entertain a crowd.

Amidst this robust merriment, the other classes come into the studio to begin their last full rehearsal at the Dance Centre, before moving their operation to the stage later this week. The Advanced dancers spread out in a large circle and sit on the floor. Randi helps the youngsters find spots between them. This is the second time they warm up like this: on the second full rehearsal and then today. It allows the small, inexperienced ones to get acclimated to being around the older ones in a bigger group. Miss Val gives the go-ahead to start and Randi leads first.

She extends her legs out in front of her and rotates her ankles one way and then the other. Everyone mimics the movements, followed by flexing and pointing. Then Todd stands up and does jumping jacks, counting loudly as the others enthusiastically join in.

Randi grins and rolls her eyes. "Whatever." And then she playfully speeds them up by counting faster.

Now they're all laughing and Annie has a heck of a time reining them back in for *pliés* and *relevés*. Julie sits down again and stretches over each leg, first pointing and then flexing. And, of course, pancake. Deanne leads *ronde de jambes,* and Brindle *frappés* into *grand battements.* Sophia tries to get them to do *chaînés* turns moving away from the circle and then back again, but they all bump into each other and end up laughing instead. Miss Val calls them back to order and Jack does complicated *pirouettes,* which, of course, even the Beginners try and most of them fall down, giggling.

"I know this is the last time we meet before dress rehearsal, and I'm glad you all are having such a good time, but we really do have to focus—so we'll be as ready as possible. *Capiche?*"

This admonition from Miss Val gets the cast into a more productive mode and they assume their starting positions for Act One, to run through the ballet in order. Jack pairs up with Randi and the young couple is supported by the villagers who are there to celebrate their upcoming nuptials. Later, when Franz flirts and shows off for the doll in the window, Jack notices how the young girls are staring at him. *Are they impressed? It looks like it.* He decides to totally get into the part and be super expressive, *for their benefit.* He smiles and hams it up and they giggle and stop dancing their parts to just watch him.

"Come on, dancers," Miss Val calls over the music. "Stay in character, everyone!"

Most of them snap to and remember their roles and the rehearsal continues for the next hour and a half. At the end, Miss Val has each group sit in certain areas to facilitate the costume distribution and parent meeting. Ms. Flanners, the costume lady, comes in the door loaded down with bright, colorful outfits wrapped in clear plastic bags. Paige and Brindle get up to help her. They bring in more hangers draped in fine attire and hook them onto the ballet *barres.*

"These are absolutely gorgeous," the teacher gushes as she pulls the skirt outward from a green peasant dress.

Ms. Flanners hangs her armload, huffing out of breath. "Thanks, Val. I was up most the night finishing these. And then I didn't bag anything until today."

"Well, it looks like you've outdone yourself, once again. Oh, I'd better let these parents in."

Moms, dads, and siblings make their way into the studio and find either sitting or standing room for the brief meeting to follow. Miss Val's really good at keeping it short and not holding anyone up for long. As she goes through her list of reminders for the dress rehearsal, the concert, and the fair performance, she asks for volunteers. "I must sound like a broken record by now, but a story ballet is much more difficult and labor intensive to put on than a regular recital would be. But, hopefully, we all get more out of it, too, including the parents."

Her captive audience agrees and a man adds, "Home of the story ballet, right?" She nods, then asks again for helpers while the costumes are handed out. Randi and Jack start talking about their plans for after the summer.

"Have you decided what you want to take this fall? I'm going to sign up for English, math, history, and hopefully at least two dance classes. Maybe ballet and contemporary. We'll see."

"Sounds ambitious," Jack mumbles, staring off into space. "I still have no idea. I'm not sure I'll even be around. I might do one of those WWOOFer programs abroad. I've applied to one for this summer, in France."

"Oohh, really?" Randi turns to face him. "Would you get to dance while you're there, too?"

"I don't know. Hopefully." He looks around the room at everyone holding their brand-new costumes and leaving with their parents. "It must be nice to know what you want to do."

"Sometimes, sometimes not, I suppose. It could be rather freeing to *not* know. And you can definitely be more spontaneous, don't you think?"

Miss Val walks across the room and starts organizing the costume rental agreements on her desk.

"Huh—I never really thought about it like that." And he hadn't. He finds he has even more things to ponder in the days leading up to the performances and after. *One thing at a time,* he tells himself.

Jack walks Randi out to her car and hops on his bike. "See you Thursday!"

"Yup—I can't wait. I, Swanilda, will marry my beloved sweetheart, Franz." She laughs at herself and waves goodbye. "Until then, my love," she teases.

What a nut. But a cute one. And she's super nice. Jack pedals along the backroads of town, feeling himself slip into the mind of his character, Franz. *Might as well, so I can deliver a more believable performance on Friday.* He chuckles down the lane, popping wheelies and behaving frivolously.

But through it all, he's slowly becoming aware of a general lightening of his mood. A sort of low-lying happiness seems to permeate his ongoing, natural state. New possibilities have opened up for him—like potential travel or a new course of study, along with those who believe in him—like Dad, Miss Val, and Randi. *Life is definitely looking up.*

18

STAGE TIME

Julie

Are you ready to take that leap? Plan well.

Julie rummages through her makeup case, trying to find the new mascara she bought last week. "Drat! Where could it be?"

"Is that it over there?" Paige asks, pointing to a small tube on the floor.

"Yes! It must have fallen out and rolled away."

Sophia picks it up and tosses it back.

"Thanks."

The girl's dressing room on the left side of the stage bustles with nerves and preparations. The dress rehearsal is to begin in forty-five minutes and there's still much to be done: hair, makeup, getting costumes on, placing accessories *just so* for everything to run smoothly and efficiently. That's not even counting what is currently being taken care of and what needs to happen onstage and backstage: lights, sound, and more. Julie flashes on what a complicated job their ballet teacher must have.

JP, Miss Val's assistant, pokes her head in the door. "Are you gals almost ready for warmups? Ooh, cute dress, Randi."

"Gettin' there, and thanks."

Julie follows Brindle, Deanne, and Sophia out to the rosin box. They're all wearing their *pointe* shoes, but she hasn't had hers long enough. She still clutches the *barre* for support. The Advanced dancers are allowed to warm up themselves with *pliés, relevés, battements...* while JP has everyone else spread out across the stage and then leads them in exercises. Each group has their own parent volunteer to help them behave and stay on task.

The guys are standing together, downstage left. Jack pulls one knee upward at a time, toward his chest, while Todd lunges sideways rather precariously. He's obviously telling a joke or something, because moments later Julie hears the three of them busting up. Mike has joined the cast again since they needed someone to play the small part of the mayor, otherwise Miss Val would have had to step in. But she has enough on her plate already.

Julie sits down to stretch next to Sophia. "I'm so tired. Cari cried so much last night I could barely sleep. I probably only got six hours—not enough."

Sophia perks up. "Well, I only got about five," she brags. "Do you want to know why?"

Julie looks sideways at her. "I wasn't aware it was a competition."

Sophia playfully spins around on her bottom. "*Mi abuela* got here last night and is staying with us!"

"Really? I thought she was so sick."

"She was," Sophia says. "But she's done with her chemo and now she's going to recover here with *mi familia*. I'm so excited."

"That's great, Sophia. I'm glad."

"Yes. She'll get to see our concert and maybe even stay for a few more weeks. I love her *so* much."

Suddenly, Julie doesn't feel quite so tired anymore. It's such a relief to see her friend this happy.

"Places, everyone!" Miss Val shouts and each group lines up to leave the stage and go to the designated areas to watch and wait for their time in the show. "And remember, let's have fun!" She smiles and enthusiastically gives a double thumbs-up.

Act One opens onto the festive village scene. Swanilda dances with her friends as well as her beloved Franz. Julie can't help but wish that someday, she, too, will be able to dance the lead in such a romantic ballet as this. *To love and be loved, even if pretending, must be spectacular.* She realizes the magic of the fairy tale is getting to her. But they've all mentioned it before—getting swept up into the story and living and breathing its life. They are each part of something bigger—becoming part of the fantasy.

Mike walks on from stage left, puffed up with authority. Randi and Jack can't help snickering at their friend's serious attitude. The mayor holds up two white sacks with big dollar signs handwritten on them with permanent marker. He's promising this dowry to the couple, which they'll receive on their wedding day.

Except for during the *pas de deux* of the betrothed couple, all the ballet dancers fill the stage. Beginners, Intermediates, and the Advanced dancers perform their own parts as well as join the others. Julie's spirits lift and she finds herself smiling effortlessly. Of course, the beautiful music by Delibes inspires the entire cast to actually *become* part of that antiquated village.

After the stage empties, night falls on the town. Instead of rats filling the street and wreaking havoc, squirrels scurry out. The little preschool gymnasts, dressed in the most adorable squirrel costumes, scuttle on from all directions. For being so young, they really seem to have it down. But maybe it's *because* they're so little, that whatever they manage to do is fantastic.

Two of them run toward each other and stop to sniff noses. A few others do lopsided summersaults across the back, due to the bulky squirrel suits. Several run higgledy-piggledy around and around the stage, while one can't seem to get over herself and stands downstage right, posing for the small, appreciative audience. Laughter takes over backstage.

"We definitely have to run this one again," Miss Val declares, and the scene is reset.

After Act One finishes, the girls retreat to the dressing room to freshen up and drink water. They need to look their best because the dress rehearsal and the concert are being filmed by the videographer and his helper. This way, the best footage from both nights can be used to create the final product the families may purchase. Julie will make sure to get one.

Before long, JP comes in again and calls them to action. The dance with the toys is one of Julie's favorites and she always startles when the trash can lid falls off one of their heads and clatters. *You'd think I'd be used to it by now. Wait, that toy isn't in costume.*

Miss Val notices, too, and stops the music. "Where's your costume? You're supposed to be wearing it now for the dress rehearsal."

The sassy preteen tells her she doesn't like it and wants to wear something else. Miss Val gets very close to her and speaks quietly. Whatever it is she says, the girl gets the message, snatches her outfit from her mom off the front of the stage, changes, and returns in less than five minutes.

Miss Val and JP are whispering to each other and nod to the girl to get back in place.

I wonder what she said? I guess Miss Val has worked her magic.

"Okay, let's start again from the top!" their leader shouts up to the booth at the back of the auditorium, above the audience. Then she turns toward the cast. "This is why we have a dress rehearsal."

Their dance with the toys begins again, and this time, runs smoothly. The curtains close and the narrator would go out now, but not tonight. They just run the rehearsal as close to how it should be as possible. When the curtains reopen, the toys tumble and Coppélia dances in front of the mats. During the lively music, Swanilda grabs the doll and drags her offstage. Dr.

Coppelius enters and the tumbling continues in the silence that follows the end of the music. But then, they all fall in a heap and the scene ends.

When the lights come back up, the mad doctor is chasing Franz around the stage using a chair as a weapon. Finally, he succeeds and the lovesick young man is thrust into the chair against his will. Julie always laughs at the part where Todd pretends to yank back Jack's head and pour the potion down his throat. Now that he's out like a light, the old man briefly goes offstage and returns, wheeling out Coppélia— but it's really Swanilda wearing the doll's clothes. Of course, Randi has her own identical costume for their performances.

Dr. Coppelius gives her a hand mirror and scarf and Randi, as the doll, mechanically dances. And then Swanilda tries to rescue her beloved Franz, realizing he's in grave danger. This is Julie's absolute favorite part. From offstage left, she watches her friends go back and forth, rise and collapse, pitch and fall. The tug-of-war ensues and Julie and Sophia laugh out loud; Miss Val shakes her head at them, putting an index finger to her lips.

When Swanilda successfully rescues Franz and they run off together, Coppelius is left with the pile of nonfunctioning toys. He now wonders what's happened to his real prize possession. He drags out another chair with a crumpled doll in it. Deanne sits lifeless, wearing only a nude-colored leotard and tights. In the story, Swanilda has made off with her clothes and the poor old man has been tricked out of his grand scheme to rob the life force from Franz and give it to his Coppélia.

In the final act, Julie smiles sweetly, as one of the bride's friends who stand on either side of the small, young dancer playing the priest. He holds a book and pretends to make his speech while Swanilda and Franz kneel before him. As soon as the curtains come up, there's laughter from the audience. It is pretty funny to have such a small priest. Miss Val said it might get a laugh when she'd cast one of the Intermediate boys. He maintains his seriousness in spite of it and the celebration continues. Mike, as the mayor, comes on with the promised bags of money for the young couple.

But the gift is not to be. Dr. Coppelius comes to them and expresses such sadness for his broken dolls that the couple feels sorry for him. After Franz pantomimes his idea to Swanilda, and she agrees, he hands the old man both sacks.

Would that ever actually happen in real life? All Julie's friends are projecting their stage personas, so she does the same.

At last pacified by the generous gift, the old man takes his leave and the *finale* begins. All the villagers dance and the toys join in the big *chassé* circle around the newly married couple. When the curtains close for the final time, it marks the end of their dress rehearsal. Miss Val has everyone sit down where they are and the stage manager opens the curtains so the parents out in the auditorium can hear her.

"Good job, everyone. Please make sure not to forget any of your things when you leave here tonight. And get them well organized for tomorrow. Call time is 5:45 and you Advanced dancers—" she looks around at them. "You need to be here no later than five, okay?"

Todd beams up at her. "Yes ma'am!"

The kids sitting near him giggle.

"Okay then. Any questions?"

As Miss Val clarifies a few details, the costume lady corrals a couple squirrels to hand-stitch their ears on better. A mom stands nearby. "They steal the show every time, don't they?"

"They sure do," Ms. Flanners says, sending one of the young rodents back to her parents.

"How did you come up with such an adorable costume idea?" Julie's mom asks, walking over.

"Oh, I don't know. I guess Val and I came up with it together somehow."

Julie pats her little sister's head. *She looks so comfy snuggled up against Mom like that. It must be nice to be that small and huggable.*

"Are you ready to go?" Mom picks up the diaper bag at her feet.

"Yes." Julie yawns and they trudge out the auditorium doors into the night. It's late for them to be out with the baby, but after all, this is their performance season. She waves to Randi and Paige, who are leaving together, and watches Sophia get into her father's car. "Will Dad make it back in time tomorrow night to see the concert?"

"He said he would. I know he wouldn't want to miss it. You all have put in so much time and hard work on this ballet. I know I'm looking forward to it tremendously."

"Thanks, Mom." Julie lightly leans her head against Mom's shoulder when they stop at the car. "I'm looking forward to it, too. It's so much fun here with these kids."

As soon as they get home, Julie gets ready for bed so she'll be at her best for the big day tomorrow.

19

COPPÉLIA

Jack

Good luck, everyone! I believe in you!

Jack watches the three musketeers, as some call the group of Deanne, Brindle, and Sophia. Julie goes over and Sophia invites her to join them in their pre-performance chant.

"It may be silly, but it's tradition," Sophia says.

Brindle welcomes her in and Deanne rolls her eyes. "Do we really have to do this *again*? It's kind of lame."

"Oh, come on. Ready?" Sophia asks, looking over at Julie.

The foursome now form a circle and Jack and Todd look on. Others take notice as well.

The girls touch hands to the side and clap out the rhythm.

"Pat a cake, pat a cake, dance if you can!
Yes ma'am, yes ma'am, of course we can!
Graceful, flowing, nailing every step!
We can, we can, dance with pep!"

When they finish, the whole cast erupts in hoots and hollers, in either support or light-hearted teasing. The girls look around, embarrassed, but JP walks through, suppressing the noise by pressing her arms downward. However, she's smiling, too.

Miss Val comes backstage after doing her last walk through the auditorium. She always does this right before their concert begins. Jack watches her nod to the stage manager, who used to be a Dance Centre student years ago but still likes to be involved. She stands downstage center, waiting to address the group.

"Well—are we ready?" She smiles and nods excitedly. "I know you all will do your best. And always remember—have fun!"

Her enthusiasm is contagious, and the volunteers take the happy little students to their starting places while all the ballet dancers assemble onstage. The narrator goes out through the break in the middle of the closed curtains to announce the ballet and tell the audience the story of *Coppélia*. This man, too, has been providing his service for the Dance Centre ballets for as long as Jack can remember. And he's funny. Even though he's dressed in a suit, he always snags someone's costume accessory for the part and this time he's got one of Coppélia's props. The elegant purple scarf is wrapped around his neck and drapes down the front of his shirt like a necktie.

He begins to reveal the fairy tale, and both the audience and cast members settle in to be transported.

"*Coppélia* is about a foolish young man who falls in love with a pretty doll named Coppélia."

That's me—the foolish young man. Jack sometimes halfway believes it, too, like right now, as the man continues to spin the tale.

"Franz, the young man, deserts his true sweetheart, Swanilda."

Randi glances over at him and grins playfully. He returns her smile and nods. *Why do I get such mixed messages from her? Sometimes it seems like she really likes me. But I know she only wants to be friends. And it's what I want too—most of the time. Ugh.* Jack struggles to pull his focus back to reality as the music begins, followed by the curtains opening.

The merriment of the occasion unfolds and Randi dances with her stage friends, bringing them all into the imagined festivities. Jack almost misses his entrance when he finds himself distracted again with his silly, shallow thoughts about girls. *Pull it together, man!*

Franz begins his flirtations with the doll in the window. Jack postures, shows off with *tour jetés* and *grand faillis*, and blows kisses—all to no avail as Deanne sits motionless in her chair behind the large window framework, staring at a book. *I'm not much better than this clueless guy. He's just thrown his beloved's feelings out the door, just to follow his next fancy. But it's not really like that with Randi. We're real friends who respect each other—aren't we?* He pulls himself back to the dance with a perfect triple *pirouette. I nailed it!*

Now in the zone, Jack dances with authority and conviction. The girls look like they belong in this village setting, over a hundred years ago. The beautiful music carries them on notes of emotion, setting the tone for each one of them. Once again, the ballet dancers are becoming one with the fairy tale as they immerse themselves deeper and deeper into that magical world.

Act One comes to an end and the narrator heads out again, this time wearing a bonnet of one of the little peasant girls. The cast can hear laughter from the audience.

When the next act begins, they seamlessly drift from scene to scene. Todd is great at being Dr. Coppelius. He has no problem whatsoever acting like a crazy old man. Jack has to work pretty hard to maintain his composure and not laugh as he pushes him around. His little sidekicks, the boys from the Intermediate class, are trying to get at the toymaker's weak points, but Todd fends them off well. With Jack's final jest, the larger-than-life key falls from his belt, and he staggers offstage.

Randi enters and dance/scolds him for harassing the old man, forcing Jack and his buddies to make an exit as well. Swanilda finds the humungous key and she and her friends conspire to break into the shop. Jack's having a blast watching the funny antics from the *sidelines,* and briefly thinks about his flip-flopping between sports language and dance terminology.

By the end of the ballet, it almost feels like he's actually getting married, albeit by a smaller-than-life priest. The couple radiates happiness and the festivities continue. Franz accepts the dowry from the mayor and turns around and gives it to Dr. Coppelius. Coppélia enters from stage right and Swanilda rises to toss her bouquet. With a lucky throw, Deanne catches it and happily twirls around.

Everyone is celebrating now and the toys *chassé* on as they embark on the finale. Jack and Randi are the last to take their bows and Randi follows with one last curtsy. The audience gives them a standing ovation and Miss Val comes out to add her own applause.

She takes the microphone. "Thank you." Turning around she blows a kiss to the cast. "Good job, you guys!" Their graceful, gracious ballet teacher begins by thanking everyone who has helped bring this production to fruition. "It certainly does take a village and each one of you is a part of it." Pink carnations are handed out to everyone in the cast, and bouquets to her "right arms," including the costume lady, stage manager, narrator, and JP.

The curtains eventually close and Jack follows Todd into the boys dressing room on stage right.

"Are you going out with us after?" Todd asks. He pulls off his smock and wanders around the small room looking for his shirt.

"Yeah. The B Street Bistro, right?"

"Mm hmm," Todd hums from underneath the T-shirt he's pulling over his head.

"But *after* the reception. We *have* to stay for that."

The two friends hurry out to the auditorium for juice and cookies. The girls, *of course*, haven't even changed yet and are holding flowers and talking in groups. They say in unison, "Figures." And then look at each other. "Jinx."

To Jack, it seems like the festivities of the actual ballet have simply shifted to the auditorium. The whole thing is surreal and he doesn't want it to end, or think about how this is the culmination of their whole year together. Four of them are seniors and will be moving on, one way or another. There's still the performance at the county fair, but this was the main one. *Why do things always have to change?*

~❦~

The group straggles, mostly together, into the bistro. Paige, Jack, and Todd had gotten a ride with Randi.

Todd pulls out a chair to sit at the largest table. "I'm starving."

"Even after all those cookies you ate?" Randi asks, sitting down across from him.

He laughs. "But I only had a few."

"More like ten," Paige corrects.

The three, no—now four musketeers are scouring the menu at the end of the table.

Brindle places both palms on the surface and stands up, clearing her throat. "I know I don't usually speak up like this, but as my mom's daughter, I'd like to congratulate all of us for such an amazing performance—and a fun one, too!" She picks up her glass of ice water. "Cheers to our ballet family."

"Yes, cheers to everyone," Paige adds and they all join in the toast.

The hungry, and not so hungry, dancers order an assortment of pizza, bread sticks, and other heavy carbs. Tonight is special. They don't *all* get together like this very often. It's a real treat.

Todd faces Jack. "Hey, how did it go at that meeting down in San Diego? Has it already been?"

"Yup. It was probably a waste of time, but I guess it was good experience."

"Well, what did you say?"

Jack thinks for a moment, trying to recall. "I talked about how Nuevo is sort of already a hub. People pass through it to get to the mountains and the desert, *and* many live here and work down the hill. You know, if we had decent public transportation up here, I think more and more commuters would use it. But I think it mostly fell on deaf ears. They all seem to want bigger and better roads."

Paige scoots closer to join the conversation. "I think it's a great idea. Sometimes things start with just a small grassroots effort. Maybe that's what it will take."

"Could that be your new purpose, Jack?" Randi nudges his shoulder.

"I don't know." He smirks at Todd. "Even this guy here has a new important purpose—Stanford!"

"Enough about me and back to you," Todd says, diplomatically.

Of course, this brings a wave of laughter since he's so good at being hilarious while looking so serious.

"Isn't it disenchanting to see how rich people and big companies can just throw money at something to get what they want? The rest of us sit by and let them do it, like we have no say at all. And it keeps being more of the same."

Brindle interrupts. "What if you major in urban planning, or something like that? Then *you* could help build a better future for all—instead of allowing the status quo to remain."

"Yeah, it's food for thought." He leans back and runs his hands through his longish hair and the first pizzas arrive.

"Which is the gluten-free one?" Paige asks.

The waitress points to the one with the most greens on top and she and Brindle nod excitedly. The other food is brought out and waters are refilled.

Annie recommends that Jack go to the local community college. "That way, you could see what you might be interested in without declaring a major first." She pecks at the tiny dinner salad in front of her.

"That's what I'm doing—and dancing, of course," Randi says.

"Of course." Deanne snickers.

"I want to keep dancing, too," Jack says. "I like that it's such a creative outlet *and* it's therapeutic."

Julie finishes chewing then agrees about dance being good therapy. "I always feel better after I dance, no matter what."

"That dance party at your house was sure fun, Randi," Sophia says.

Jack had heard about it. It did sound like a lot of fun. "And you know what else is so cool about dance?" He looks around the table at them. "That it's this beautiful art form that doesn't take up any space to store or contribute to our civilization's accumulation of stuff." He grins at the end of his proclamation.

Paige adds, "And it doesn't add to global warming."

"What about all our sweat?" Todd asks. "Doesn't that warm up the planet?"

They all crack up.

"Here, here!" Brindle raises her glass again and they do another toast.

"To dance!" they all sing.

"So—" Todd steers the topic back. "Urban planning?"

"Maybe, but first I think I need to learn more about public transportation—and life." He chuckles. "It turns out I got approved to be a WWOOFer at a small urban farm in France—for the summer. I should be able to experience their mass transit firsthand."

"That's great. Congratulations!" Annie says. And this starts another group round of "Cheers."

Somehow, mixed in with the other voices, Jack senses his mom. He smiles and thinks that maybe, just maybe, he *is* making her proud. The thought floods him with warm feelings and he's grateful to be celebrating with his friends—right now.

The tired but satisfied dancers eat their fill and talk openly, their conversation flowing fluidly from one topic to the next. Jack likes sitting next to Randi. It feels good to be her friend, and he hers. Their relationship is uncomplicated and relaxed. He realizes it's always a choice—to be fickle like Franz or to live with integrity and purpose, *and* to live a balanced life. This is what it will mean to be Jack, he decides.

They all stand up to say their goodbyes and when Jack turns to leave, Randi plants a kiss on his cheek. She quickly smiles and heads toward the door. It makes him start to wonder—all over again.

20

Grunion Run

Julie

Go ahead, run barefoot in the sand.

The Dance Centre's performance of *Coppélia* at the county fair has come and is almost finished. The last act is just over and Julie starts thinking about summer. Hopefully, she'll get to go to that dance camp in LA. Mom hasn't completely decided yet. As she grasps Willow's arm, the sequins on their sleeves catch. Since they're dancing in the large group with all the Advanced, Intermediate, and Beginning ballet students, it probably isn't all that noticeable to the audience. But she remains hooked to Miss Val's younger daughter's arm and can't wriggle free.

Willow shoots her a worried look and Julie whispers, "On three?"

On the third count, they yank away from each other, a little too forcefully, and now a long, sparkly strand hangs from Julie's sleeve. *Whatever, it's not the end of the world.* She joins the other Advanced girls behind Randi and within minutes the wedding ceremony is performed and the dowry exchanges have taken place. The *finale* celebration culminates and the cast bows as a group.

Except there's a problem. Julie can't come up from hers. The segment from Willow's sleeve, which has now become part of hers, has caught on both the skirt and bodice, trapping Julie in place. *Great—now what? On three again? What if my whole dress rips apart right here in the middle of the stage? It's not like I'm wearing a leotard underneath or anything. Ugh!*

As the others rise up and down again for the next bow, Julie remains bent over, looking pathetic. She uses her fingers to try to untangle the mess, but it's useless. *What's a poor girl to do?* She shakes her head in dismay while hanging upside down, feeling sorry for herself. She swings from side to side and all of a sudden, the thread gives way and unravels—freeing one part of the fabric from the other. She can finally stand up with the rest of them and Sophia nods to the front of her dress. It's all frayed, but at least intact. Julie grimaces while the crowd applauds under the billowy netting above the Showcase Stage area.

The dancers head back toward the dressing room tents behind the stage to change into street clothes so they can return their rental costumes. When Julie points out the torn fabric on the front of her costume, Miss Val tells her not to worry.

"These things happen. I saw it, both times. Willow's sleeve is pretty messed up, too." In spite of this, she shrugs and says she's looking forward to seeing her this summer, or at least in the fall. JP walks over with a question, and Julie goes to find Sophia.

The two girls plan to hang out at the fair, going on rides and checking out some of the exhibits. Later, Sophia's parents will pick them up to go to the beach with their family. But first, cotton candy!

When Julie takes her first bite, half of it falls off the stick onto the ground. "Oh man—no way!"

Sophia shakes her head. "You're not having very good luck today, are you? First your costume and now this?" She giggles playfully and wags her finger warningly. "You best be on your toes for the rest of the day, girl."

"I guess I better." She knows her friend is just teasing, though, and it's good to see her this lighthearted since her grandmother's arrival.

Brindle and Deanne come up from behind and invite them to come meet the others at the big roller coaster, if they'd like.

"Okay. That sounds fun," Sophia says.

Julie agrees and the foursome hurries through the crowds to the center of the midway.

"How long are you guys staying?" Paige asks when they meet up.

"Until nine. How about you guys?" Sophia throws her empty cotton candy stick into the trashcan near the line.

"Us, too," Brindle answers, looking up at the highest rise of the roller coaster.

Randi is giving Paige, Jack, and Todd rides home, so they're not sure yet.

"No Annie?" Julie asks.

"No. She never stays after. That girl's got one busy schedule, that's for sure." Todd grins with pleasure when the rattly roller coaster careens past them.

Julie's stomach starts doing summersaults in anticipation of the wild ride. "I hope I don't fall out." She grimaces.

Sophia overhears. "Are you concerned about your bad luck today? Don't worry, I was just teasing. This is going to be a blast!"

When they reach the front of the line, the dancers board the cars two-by-two: Randi and Jack; Paige and Todd; Brindle and Deanne; and finally, Julie and Sophia.

The miniature train jerks into motion and Todd looks back. "Here we go. May the fun begin!"

At the very top, Julie closes her eyes and holds on for dear life. She grits her teeth, but can't help screaming anyway. And there's a lot of screaming—from all around. Her body is slammed from side-to-side and sometimes bumps into Sophia. They both shriek at every turn and at the very end—they all want more. Even though it's a good fifteen-minute wait, they do it over and over again. While they stand in line, it gives them a chance to find out what each other is doing over the summer.

"I'm off to France in a week!" Jack declares.

"Lucky duck," Paige says. "I'm moving up to Berkeley to stay with my sister until school starts."

Randi reminds them she'll be going to the community college, and taking general ed courses and as many dance classes as she can fit into her schedule. Todd plans on continuing his job at the rental place until a week before Stanford starts.

"I'm still hoping my mom will let me go to that dance camp in LA." Julie knows Brindle and Deanne will be there.

Sophia is the most excited. "*Mi abuela* is staying with us and I want to spend as much time with her as possible."

At a quarter to nine, they make their way to the parking lot. Julie hasn't been to the beach at night in a long time and wonders what it will be like spending time with Sophia's family.

By the time they arrive at La Jolla Shores, it's 9:30. The full moon has already come up and appears fuzzy in the light fog. Sophia's dad and her grandmother have already been here for quite a while and sit around the blazing fire ring. A pot of beans simmers on a grate off to the side and the old lady has a bowl of dough in her lap.

Sophia hugs her and introduces Julie to "*Abuela*."

Julie says hello and asks, "What's in there?"

Sophia starts to translate, but her grandmother seems to have understood.

"For tortillas. You help?"

"May I?" She sees Sophia has already stepped in, so she kneels down by the fire and accepts a ball of dough. She mashes it hard between her palms, but it only gets to the size of a small pancake.

The grandmother looks like a master tortilla maker as she quickly slaps an amazingly thin sheet of dough from hand-to-hand. "Like *thees*."

Sophia's ball has also flattened nicely. "No. You don't want to mash it."

Ms. Hernandez comes over to the fire after getting her four little boys settled on a blanket with their toy trucks. "It's more like tossing it back and forth, wouldn't you say?" She looks to her daughter.

"Mm hmm." Sophia starts another one for Julie and then hands it to her.

Abuela reaches over and guides Julie's hands to work "with" the dough, instead of "against" it.

The pliable substance slowly begins to grow, flatter and bigger, and she starts to get the hang of it. "There's a real knack to this, isn't there?"

"Just like everything," Sophia's mom says.

Mr. Hernandez stands up to rekindle the fire. "So, Julie—have you ever been to a grunion run before?"

She shakes her head and gets another ball from the bowl. "No. I hadn't even heard of it before Sophia invited me."

"We try to do it every year—"

Sophia interrupts. "It's like a family tradition."

He laughs. "It is. Every year, the grunion come to spawn here at high tide. Sometimes there's thousands and thousands of them, but other times there's hardly any." He adds another log to the fire. "We'll see about tonight."

After all the tortillas are made, *Abuela* says she'll stay by the fire and watch their things. "*¿Es casi la hora?*"

Julie glances out at the pounding surf and wonders how on earth they could possibly tell.

"Maybe so," he says. "Get your buckets, boys."

Sophia hands a plastic bucket to Julie. "Let's go!"

The two of them hurry down to the surf, but Julie slows down. "It's so dark. Maybe I should go back and get my phone for a flashlight."

"No," Sophia says. "That will scare the fish." She slows down so her friend can keep up.

Julie stops and stares when they get to the shallow water. Her eyes have adjusted to the moonlight and when each wave recedes, the sand shines silver with glimmering motion. "Are those fish?" She stands dumbfounded.

"Ha! They sure are. There are tons of them tonight!"

Sophia's brothers run around grabbing the poor little helpless fish squirming in the sand and plop them into their toy buckets.

Julie watches her friend pick up one wriggling specimen and place it into her pail.

"Isn't there a tool or something we can use, instead of picking them up with our hands?" She's a little squeamish about handling live, slippery fish.

"No. This is best. Come on, Julie—it's fun. You'll see."

Julie bends down to pick one up, but it drops out of her hand and she shrieks. Sophia has gone on to collect more, so Julie tries again. But first, she watches one burrow tail-first into the sand while another wraps around the spot. *Spawning. Of course. I hope most of them actually make it.* There are other people on the beach hunting grunion, too, but at least it's not very crowded. When the next wave brings in more grunion, she reaches down, wraps her hand around a small slippery body, and brings it up to her bucket. It writhes around, but she tries not to think about it and joins the party.

After about an hour of catching, squealing, and running to the next wave, the group retreats back to the fire ring with their loot. Mr. Hernandez has them all dump their fish into a larger pail so he can clean them. Julie looks on as he cuts off their heads and tails on a chopping block, one-by-one. Then Sophia's mom coats them in oil. *Abuela* has been cooking tortillas and reminds them to use lime juice and chile powder while they're grilling.

As their late dinner cooks, Julie and Sophia walk around the small folding table displaying the taco garnishes. Lettuce, tomatillos, green onions, salsa, grated cheese, cilantro, tomatoes, guacamole, and radishes make Julie's stomach growl. Then she remembers the pot of beans on the fire and can't wait for the delicious food.

"It's going to be quite a feast, huh?" She's amazed at the preparation that must have gone into this.

Ms. Hernandez passes out paper plates to the boys and helps them load their tacos. Sophia's dad is almost finished grilling the last of the grunion and *Abuela* nods to Julie to try one. She holds out her plate and a small, crisp-looking morsel is dropped onto it. She gingerly picks it up with her fingers and takes a tiny bite.

"Well?" Sophia asks, smiling.

"Mmm, not too bad." The salty, crunchy, lemony flavor floods her tastebuds and she realizes it's actually quite good. "I like it."

"Of course, you do." Sophia laughs. "They're wonderful."

The girls take fresh, warm tortillas from the foil on the side of the grill and a few fish. Julie layers the condiments from the table into her taco and dishes up a ladleful of beans on the side. She and Sophia settle onto a large blanket laid out on the sand and partake in one of the most original and fun meals she's ever experienced.

"Do you guys really do this *every* year?"

"Just about," Sophia answers. "And *Abuela* almost always comes, too." She looks over at her grandmother and the old lady smiles back, eyes twinkling.

"These are *so* good."

"We think so," Ms. Hernandez says from her chair over by the boys. "We keep coming back for more."

The group laughs and Sophia's dad leans over to his mother and whispers something in Spanish. She grins and nods.

They look so happy—and relaxed. I wish our family could do more stuff together like this. They're all so close. Julie sets her plate in her lap and leans back on her elbows. The moon has moved almost to its zenith and the beach glows around them. A few campfires burn nearby, but not too close.

Julie pictures her mom, and little Cari, in a setting like this. And Dad, too. *Yeah, it's possible. Especially if I stop being a sourpuss about helping out.* She thinks about how she *is* actually *doing* more things now, and watching a little less anime—as well as being more discriminating about which ones she watches. And how, especially after that trip to Mexico, they all get along better and seem to find more time for each other.

Having Sophia for a friend has helped me learn more about the value of family. And, now that I think about it, I have a pretty good one, too. I'm going to tell them as soon as I get home tonight—or rather, this morning.

ACKNOWLEDGEMENTS

Any work of this type requires a village. That is to say, that without the help of everyone involved, this book would not have come to fruition. My dear friends who provided editing, ideas, and support include Helen Buchanan, Bo Varnado, Kent Richardson, Justice Choate, Beverly Silvers, and numerous friends and ballerinas. For the business of getting this book published I'd like to thank Monkey C Media. A special appreciation goes to Pamela Wilder for providing the wonderful cover art. And to my children: Jessie, Kali, and Chance. There are also many more kind souls who have helped bring this project to completion—you know who you are. And last, but not least, to my husband, Kent, for his ongoing belief in my abilities as a writer.

ABOUT THE AUTHOR

Chi Varnado lives in the backcountry of San Diego County with her husband and a menagerie of animals. She taught dance for thirty-seven years and her own studio staged a story ballet each year—similar to the one in *The Dance Centre Presents Coppélia*! This novel is Miss Chi's sixth published book, the third in the series, *The Dance Centre Presents*. Visit us at DanceCentrePresents.com.